Lord Haversham Takes Command

A Miss Delacourt Adventure

HEIDI ASHWORTH

ISBN-13: 978-0615827049
Dunhaven Place Publishing

By the same author:

Miss Delacourt Speaks Her Mind
Miss Delacourt Has Her Day
Lady Crenshaw's Christmas
A Timeless Romance Anthology: Winter Collection:
It Happened Twelfth Night

For Harry—
he knows who he is.

Contents

chapter one

"La! How dowdy are the *de rigueur* fashions from *La Belle Assemblee,* circa eighteen twelve!" exclaimed Miss Miranda Crenshaw. "I declare, if I were forced to wear such a bonnet, I would spend my days below stairs washing-up with the scullery maid!"

Her father, seated by the fire at Prospero Park, the country seat of the Crenshaw clan, allowed his copy of *The Examiner* to slip as far as the arch of his nose so as to serve his wife a speaking look.

She returned his look with a twinkle in her eyes. "Now, Mira, as I have said on numerous occasions . . ."

"I should think 'multifarious' a more apt word than 'numerous,' Mama," Mira said with a pert air. "Though 'copious' and 'profuse' would do just as well."

"Very well, then," her mother demurred. "I shall always applaud the superior word, no matter how disagreeably it is thrust within my notice. But that is neither here nor there." She dropped her needlework into her lap and heaved a sigh. "I do not recollect what I was about to say."

Mira opened her mouth to rehearse the oft-used phrase, but her father was quicker.

"Well-bred young ladies do not prattle on about tawdry subjects such as clothing, except when in the company of their dressmaker," he intoned. "Well-bred and dashing gentlemen are under no such stricture, however," he added with a deft duck of his head beneath the paper before Lady Crenshaw could pin him with a gimlet glare.

Mira stood, allowing the relics of her mother's debutante season to slip from her lap to the floor, and went to peer out the window. "I don't know why you are so prosy on the subject, *ma mere.* Clothes and fashion are all my friends speak of. That is, except for Viola, who is prodigious intelligent and converses on any manner of subjects of which I've never heard."

"And it is no accident that she, as your sole respite from girlish frivolity, is your bosom beau. And then there are your brothers. Think what mayhem might ensue should they put too much stock in what they put on their backs."

"Stephen and Adrian?" Mira cried. "Why, they would don nightshirts for Queen Victoria's ball if it weren't for my constant admonitions. I hardly think they are the epitome of stylish restraint."

"S'true. There's barely a Brummell between them," Sir Anthony mumbled from behind the society page.

"What was that, dearest?" Lady Crenshaw asked with an exasperated air.

"Oh, do leave off twitting him, Mama," Mira cried as she dashed to her father's side and knelt at his feet. "You must own you would find it as tragic as I if he were to dismiss his tailor and dress like a country squire."

Lady Crenshaw pointedly pursed her lips and retrieved her needle and hoop. "Very well then, I shall leave off the subject of clothing and move on to that display of histrionics instead."

"Ginny, my love," Sir Anthony said with a toss of his paper. "We knew when the girl made her entrance with that head of flaming red hair that she would display a goodly amount of dramatic flair. If you must blame someone, blame Grandmama, the original redheaded termagant, who is dead and well past caring."

"I could more easily blame you," Lady Crenshaw said under her breath, "if she weren't my relative as well as yours! There, that's done it," she announced with a snap of the thread between her teeth.

"Why, it's the prettiest monogrammed hankie I've seen yet." Sir Anthony rose to his feet and took the bit of muslin in his hand to examine the intricately entwined A and G. "I shall make a point of taking too much snuff at the next affair we attend so as to bring your handiwork to the attention of all assembled. I am sure to be the envy of each and every one," he said with a bow and a kiss for his lady.

Mira noted how her mother blushed under her father's gaze and hastily turned away. Sometimes she wished her parents were more circumspect, more discreet, more . . . ordinary. Their obvious affection for each other was disturbing in the extreme. "Well then, if you two lovebirds are going to continue making eyes at each other, I believe I shall go in search of my brothers."

"Not at home," her father said in an off-hand manner, his attention no doubt taken up with the tracing of circles along the skin of her mother's hand with his thumb.

"Where are they off to so early in the afternoon?" Mira asked in a huff.

"Harry is returned, hadn't you heard?" Lady Crenshaw replied. "They're off to Avery Abbey to see him."

"Without me? Not today! I shall have a thing or two to say about that when they return. Why, one would think this was not my coming out, what with this continual belittlement of my person," Mira said, a bit more loftily than she intended. She suspected her nose tilted a bit closer to the ceiling than she intended as well, but as her parents proved bereft of speech, there was nothing to do but make the best of it and sweep from the room.

Mira heard their powers of speech return in force once she slammed the drawing room door behind her, but she daren't give them the satisfaction of listening through the keyhole. She had been down that road before, and it had brought her nothing but a sound swat on the bottom from Mrs. Bell, the housekeeper. Besides, more likely than not, they even now bemoaned their lot as parents to a hoyden who could ride and shoot as well as any man, with a redhead's temperament to boot. The fact that she was in possession of a purely feminine figure, danced like a doyen, and exhibited exquisite taste in clothing seemed to impress them not one whit.

And then it hit her; Harry was home! Harry—*her* Harry! The one who in days past rode and swam and fished beside her, who swung her round in his arms at the end of each term home from school; the one who had been almost like a brother to her, at least until that day he had kissed her and she had slapped his face. She was all of twelve at the time; surely he must have forgiven her by now! As she raced up the stairs to her bedroom, she cudgeled her brain for the perfect ensemble to don for his return.

What would a gentleman recently returned from the Grand Tour in Europe find sophisticated enough without it seeming as if she were aching to impress him? The fact that she possessed a clothespress brim-full of new gowns, outfits, and fripperies hardly mattered as he hadn't laid eyes on her in almost four years nor any of her clothes in all that time. Feeling confident, she chose a sapphire blue gown and quickly donned it with the help of the tweeny who, in the somewhat economical home of Lady Crenshaw, did double duty as a body servant.

With its off-the-shoulder neckline, puffed sleeves, and split skirt that revealed a quantity of frothy white lace skimming over a delectably full petticoat, Mira felt it the height of fashion and sophistication. It was, perhaps, a bit daring for daytime wear but the fact that the sun shone could not be helped. What mattered was that the gown was the precise shade of blue as her eyes and that it complemented the cascade of red, glossy ringlets that spilled out of her chip straw bonnet to perfection.

Satisfied with her reflection in the pier glass, she tightened the belt at her satisfactorily tiny waist, took up her pocketbook in case they had a mind to go shopping in the village, and made her way below stairs to join her parents in the drawing room.

"You look ravishing, my child," Sir Anthony said as he took her in his arms and dropped a kiss on her forehead. "'Twould be a pity if he chooses not to call on us this afternoon. However, I am persuaded he is probably off cutting up some lark with your brothers."

Mira gave her father, who, she noticed, had changed into his favorite day suit, a conciliatory smile. Even Mama had removed her everyday lace cap in favor of one trimmed with the finest Venetian lace composed of a riot of cunningly worked roses. Surely, Mira thought, they were as expectant of Harry's arrival as she.

To her delight, it wasn't long before the strike of riding boots against the flagstone walkway followed by gales of masculine laughter in the front hall could be heard from the drawing room. Suddenly, Mira was all aflutter at the thought of seeing him. Once she looked into his face, however, seeing him was all she could bring herself to do.

His hair was as blond as ever, a circumstance difficult to avoid in light of his parents' fair locks, and his full lips perhaps a bit thinner than when he was a boy, though they sat above the very same divot in his chiseled chin. His nose was long and straight and a bit blunt at the end, just as she remembered, and his eyes the same intense green orbs. For a moment he favored her with the heat of his gaze from beneath the cover of a fringe of dark lashes, then strode right past her without not so much as a how-do-you-do.

"Sir Anthony, Lady Crenshaw," he said, as he greeted her parents with all the enthusiasm she felt ought to have been reserved for herself. His voice was deeper than she recalled and a bit more brittle as well. His smile was a shade too bright and his entire manner somewhat . . . off. What could possibly account for it?

Mentally, she went over her entire ensemble and knew herself to look absolutely exquisite from the crown of her ribboned bonnet to the tips of her square-toed shoes. With a confidence she felt deep in the marrow of her bones, she marched to the fireplace where their guest basked in the glow of the Crenshaw family, edged her way between her brothers, and thrust her hand beneath Harry's nose.

"I believe you have not properly greeted me," she said with a perfectly polished smile.

Harry's eyes opened wide in surprised. "If it isn't little Miss Crenshaw!" he exclaimed with an audible gasp. "I must own, I had not recognized you under that bonnet. I thought you a caller just arrived!"

Mira was certain he was lying; certain, too, the look he had given her when he entered was one of recognition, as well as something else she couldn't quite identify. Yet, he denied it all as he coyly covered his grinning lips instead of taking up the hand she held out for his kiss. At the same time, he used his other hand to fan his face with a flutter of his fingers in a gesture so unmanly as to unnerve her.

"Why, you've been allowed to let down your skirts and pin up your hair!" With a bark of laughter, he turned to her parents. "What's the occasion?"

Mira noted how round her mother's eyes had become and how her father looked, quite simply, agog, and rushed to reply before her parents made a remark that might cause her further humiliation. "It's my come-out this year, Harry. You can't have forgotten I am ten and eight come June! I shall soon be making my bows to the Queen," she said with a little pirouette.

"It's *Bertie*," her eldest brother, Stephen, said with a grimace. He and Harry had been born within months of each other the spring following their respective parents' nuptials.

"Bertie?" Mira asked looking about her for another young man who had ostensibly slipped into the house beneath her notice. "I'm afraid I don't know to whom you're referring," she said with a glance at her parents who looked to be more and more alarmed with each moment that passed.

"Poor child, I can see we have confused you," Harry purred. "It is I! That is to say, I am he—Bertie! Harry was the pseudonym of my youth, but Bertie is the *sobriquet* by which I shall be known forthwith!"

Adrian, Mira's elder brother by two years, frowned. "But your name, as I recall, isn't Albert or Bertram!"

Harry gave another bark of laughter and touched Adrian lightly on the arm as if they shared some amusing secret. "The name with which my parents graced me upon my birth was Herbert, though if I had been known as such at Eton," he gushed with an exaggerated waggle of his brows, "I would have been thrashed within an inch!"

More laughter followed though Mira couldn't help but notice that Harry—that was to say, Bertie—laughed alone. She realized he wasn't *Harry* at all, and her heart sank. As the scales fell from her eyes, she suddenly saw her former friend in a new light. Though it was true that not much about his face had altered, his taste in clothes had undergone a sea change.

Gone were the sensible but attractive and masculine clothes usually worn by Harry, now replaced by the ruffled shirt front, wide-spread collar, and tightly cinched waist favored, apparently, by those of 'Bertie's' stamp. She was most alarmed by the fact that he sported not one but two waistcoats, both quite loud and in such contrasting hues it made her more than a little dizzy to gaze upon them. Mira knew it to be all the crack of fashion, but she felt the overall look not suitable paired with riding boots and certainly too fine for the middle of the afternoon, whereupon she remembered her own unwillingness to dress in accordance with the time of day and, with a self-conscious blush, turned away.

"Well!" Lady Crenshaw cried with what Mira knew to be fabricated enthusiasm. "It is so good to see you, Harry. That is to say, *Bertie.* It would seem your years on the Continent have wrought wondrous changes in you."

Mira felt 'wondrous' to be a more appropriate description than 'wonderful'. She knew she was expected to follow her mother's comment with a request that their guest be seated and regale them with tales of his tour through France, Italy, and Spain, but she couldn't bring herself to do so. In point of fact, the sooner this imposter wearing Harry's face departed the better. She wandered to the other side of the room and ran her fingers along the furnishings in an absent-minded way, a clear indication she was no longer interested in socializing.

Bertie-not-Harry acknowledged her disinterest with a little cough into his fist and with gratifying speed announced his intention to depart. He said his farewells to her parents and brothers then strolled up behind her where she stood with her face to the wall as she scrutinized a painting she had seen every day of her life. He said not a word, but she could feel the agitation rise from him like a haze of heat. The thought came to her that he was more himself, more *Harry,* at this moment than any other since he first entered the room. Still, she refused to turn about and face him, afraid of what she might see, or not, if she were to look again into his eyes.

With a bray of laughter, he was off to the front hall where he made a noisy show of collecting his hat, gloves, and riding whip. However, these sounds were not immediately followed by those of his boots as they marked his way to the door, and Mira had the oddest sensation he was loathe to depart. With a surge of remorse, she brushed past her appalled parents and into the front entry where she found him still at the hall table, hatted and gloved but not gone. She thought she could see the old Harry in the rigid lines of his back, in the way he gripped the edge of the table with his long fingers, and she was certain it was Harry who threw a furtive glance over his shoulder to find her staring at him. He laughed, a rueful, Harry sort of laugh, then spun about to properly bid her goodbye.

"Miss Crenshaw," he chirped and sketched a bow. "It was a delight!" He touched the brim of his hat with his finger and favored her with a decided smirk, but it was the old Harry's eyes that lingered on her face as if he savored the very sight of her. In spite of the carefree grin, those eyes were tinged with regret.

Mira felt her heart gripped with grief. What could have happened to Harry to make him disappear? How could she beckon his return? Her brothers appeared and as 'Bertie' slapped them on the shoulders in farewell and made his way out the door, she wanted to run after him and force him to explain—to tell her where he had taken her Harry—but something held her back, and he was soon mounted and had cantered away.

Mira returned to the drawing room in time to hear her father's reaction. "Lord save us, he's the spitting image of his mother!"

"Whatever can you mean?" Lady Crenshaw cried. "He's precisely like his father!"

Sir Anthony dragged a shaking hand across his face. "Ginny, surely you saw how his hands were itching to come together in a resounding clap just like that infernal Lady Avery, and incessantly, I might add." He collapsed into his chair by the fire, for all the world like a man harassed past bearing. "I'll be hanged if there wasn't a lisp hovering about waiting for the perfect moment to be unleashed as well." He looked up at his wife. "You know what this means, don't you?"

"No! Surely you don't mean it! He wasn't as awful as all that, was he?" she asked in a voice that quavered just a trifle.

Mira felt a new and unfamiliar sensation grip her. "Papa, what are you saying?" she demanded while doing her best to hide her fear. "How does Harry's bizarre metamorphosis into Bertie have anything to do with you?"

Her mother turned haggard eyes to her daughter. "Only that you shall be expected to marry your cousin after all."

"Who?" Mira demanded. "Not George!" An uncomfortable silence ensued. A bit deflated by their lack of reply, she carried on. "You *can't* mean that I should marry George. He's the most despicable, needle-nosed tyrant who ever walked the earth! Besides, I still have no idea what this has to do with Harry." She blinked back a sudden onset of tears. She didn't know what her tears had to do with Harry either, but she refused to examine that question further.

Her father sighed and took her hand in his. "Mira, my love, we have often thought you had feelings for Harry."

"Well, yes, I suppose I might have had," Mira said in spite of her hesitation. "But you know that we have always been nothing but friends. Besides, he is *miles* older than I."

He is a mere three years older, very close to the number of years between your father and I," her mother pointed out.

"The two of you have always gotten along so well, and Harry has been almost one of the family. I can't say, however, that I have always favored the match; his parents are so . . . well, I suppose I have said too much already."

"His parents?" Mira conjured up an image of Lord Avery, Harry's corpulent father, with his long locks of gray and those tiny eyes pinched between the fat of his cheeks and that of his brow. He was forever gushing over the ladies as if he were the most eligible bachelor on the town and regularly recited the most appalling poetry. True, he was an earl, but that in no way compensated for the constant creak of his corset.

Of course Mira's father was correct with regards to Lady Avery. She had a most annoying habit of clapping her hands and never at a time that remotely warranted it. She once clapped her hands as giddily as a schoolgirl when supper at Prospero Park was announced. It had not been an interminable wait nor was it a special occasion, merely a tedious Tuesday meal of bread and mutton, but Lady Avery had clapped her hands as if it were Father Christmas come to call. It caused Mira to wonder if perhaps Lady Avery was not in possession of an average intelligence. In short, there wasn't much either of his parents had to say or think or opine that she would favor with a moment's credit.

"Yes, well . . ." her mother hedged, "it isn't as if they are any great friends of ours, and naturally it isn't only because he is an earl and she a countess," she added with what Mira felt unnecessary emphasis. "It's just as your father said; we always thought you fond of him. And," she added in a small voice, "he was better than George."

Mira cocked her head and tried to form a bitterless reply. "Yes, I do recall that he *was* better than George. Pray tell, why should he be favored for my hand in marriage whether Harry came up to scratch or not?"

"Oh, Mira!" her mother scolded. "Why such vulgar language when you have every word in the English language at your command? That being said, I insist your father address that question." And with that she turned away and paced to the other side of the room.

Sir Anthony gave his daughter a look that bordered on sheepish and cleared his throat. "You see, child, until George was born, I was next in line for the old Duke's title, he being my uncle and I his only living heir. When I married your mother, it was with the understanding that she would one day be my duchess . . ."

"Duchess, I declare!" Lady Crenshaw cried, spinning about. "You know well enough how little I cared for such things!"

"Yes, yes, 'tis true," Sir Anthony said as he shot his wife a barely concealed look of adoration. "Your mother didn't care to be a duchess nor I a duke, but the possibility was there. So, when my uncle recovered from a long illness from which he was expected to expire and suddenly took a new wife, it wasn't long until a son came along to replace the one he had lost only a short time before."

"George," Mira said.

Lord Crenshaw cleared his throat again. "Yes, George. Before my uncle finally did shuffle off this mortal coil, he insisted that the two of you should wed."

Adrian and Stephen shot to their feet, their faces alive with disgust, and quit the room. Their departure was followed by a loud sniff from her mother, causing Mira to wonder if there were more to the story than what was being said.

"But it was just a moment ago you suggested *Harry* and I were to wed," Mira replied in a leading fashion designed to produce elucidation.

"Exactly. Insisting that you were meant for Harry was the most effective way at your tender age—I believe you were only ten or eleven years old at the time—to stave off George's father," her mother said with a sigh. "As matters stood, he was already far too involved with your upbringing. Had he reason to doubt that one day you would be anything but Duchess of Marcross, his demands would have proved intolerable, up to and including your removal from our home so as to be under his very nose. To think that anyone would suppose I should allow my daughter to be raised by that woman . . ."

Again Mira felt as if there was much left unsaid, but she sensed the subject was a painful one and, as such, did not push for further explanations.

"I see. So, if I am not to wed Harry—and who should wish to?" she asked with a voice that choked a little—"then I am all but promised to George, whom I despise with hatred unabated!"

For once her mother did not scold her for exaggerating the case. "Not exactly, however, that is the light in which George sees things. I must say that we fully expected the matter to be dropped when the old Duke died, but it would seem George has decided you are his due, and I'm afraid he is rather accustomed to his wishes being fulfilled."

"But Mother, how could you? You, who would settle for nothing less than a love match! Don't you wish for me what you have with Father?" she cried as if her parents' devotion to one another had never been anything but altogether appealing and desirable. "Papa, what have you to say to this piece of nonsense?"

"Only that I, like your mother, want what's best for you."

Lady Crenshaw went to her daughter's side and put her arms about her. "Mira, when I married your father, I was twenty years old and firmly on the shelf. What's more, my father was a vicar. Your father, however, is grandson, nephew, and heir to a duke. Naturally we wanted to look high for you. In that respect, as well as many others, Harry seemed the perfect choice. As the Viscount Haversham and the son of an earl, he is a fitting match for you in spite of your lack of title. The fact that you clearly adored him put an end to our anxiety over the matter."

"Adored him," Mira mused as she slipped from her mother's arms and went to the window that afforded the last view of Harry, the one from which he had ridden away four years prior. "Yes, I did adore him," she murmured, "but *Harry* is no more."

chapter two

Harry rode away from the only place he had ever known true happiness and cursed himself for a fool. "Make that a fool twice over," he muttered aloud, though there was no one present to hear him. It was foolish to run away from her, even more foolish to think he could hide anything from her—his darling, astute, and, in every way, adorable Mira. There was a part of him that hoped he would find her so altered he could no longer bring himself to love her. He uttered a harsh laugh at the thought. Not only was she just as genuine and impetuous as ever, she was superior in so many ways—even more lovely, more brilliant, and to his mingled admiration and horror, more perceptive. How could he have thought for a single moment he could manage to carry out his plans under her very nose? The only sensible answer was to steer clear of his heart's desire though that same heart quailed at the thought.

He must play out this charade for as many weeks as necessary, even if it meant she might never know how much he loved her, had loved none but her his whole life long. Worse, after this afternoon's work, she would not care. How could she? If he were to execute his plan, he would be obliged to behave exactly as did his giddy mother and arrogant father. It was too dangerous to do otherwise. But how could Mira love such a man as he now appeared to be, a man with no care in the world but his privileged place in society and the quantity of lace at his throat? Lace! He couldn't abide the stuff!

With a savage kick to his undeserving mount, he broke into a gallop and streaked back to the Abbey in hopes he would have time to renew his cursedly fussy toilette and be out again for the evening before his Lord and Lady returned from wherever it was that had kept them occupied for the afternoon—not that there was much divertissement to be had in the country. It would prove easier to avoid a cozy evening by the fire with his parents once the Season had begun and they had all taken up residence at Haversham House in London.

The thought of the Season brought fresh miseries to mind. This was to be Mira's come-out, and there was no doubt of the approbation she would stir in the hearts of many. How would 'Bertie' stack up against the suitors who would vie for her hand? And how could Harry possibly abide the ever present George, Duke of Marcross, for even a moment? Memories of his arrogant disposition paired with an obsequious air filled Harry with revulsion, but there was no hope of escape if he intended to stay close to the Crenshaw clan.

With a sigh, he admitted he must devise a way to tolerate George, as avoiding Mira was out of the question. What's more, it was beyond his power. He knew it was swimming in deep water to attempt to win the heart and hand of his beloved while he maintained his cover in fulfillment of his mission, but the alternative did not bear thinking on. He had long thought it could never be—that he was unworthy of

Mira— and had resolved to stay away from Prospero Park at any cost. Her brothers, however, had cajoled him into a visit, and now that he had seen her, spoken with her, he couldn't give her up any more than he could the air he breathed.

Upon his arrival at the Abbey, he barely looked up as he tossed the reins to the groom and wearily made his way inside with few thoughts other than to take a long bath and to make an early night of it without his mother and father discovering his whereabouts. However, in that he was sorely disappointed.

"Herbert!" his mother cried the moment he stepped into the house. The fact that she pronounced his name 'air-bear' was all of a piece. "We have been at *point non plus wondering* where you could possibly be!" Her ladyship's penchant for French words and phrases made Harry's ears hurt, but escape via another Grand Tour of the continent was not within the realm of possibility. "But here you are!"

Harry sighed in anticipation of the hand clap, but it would seem he was to be spared that particular annoyance for the time being.

"Yes, Mother, I am arrived," he said and submitted himself to his mother's noisy kisses.

"See, my lord? He is home, and so are we!" she cried.

"Yes, my petal, I see that," his father said with a patience Harry knew he did not feel. "Good afternoon, Haversham. Did you find the Crenshaws in good health this fine day?"

Harry detached himself from his mother's clingy embrace and went to his father to give him the obligatory handshake, the one they always shared whether they had been parted six months or six minutes. "They are very well, Father, very well indeed." It was on the tip of his tongue to add how well he found Mira in particular, but he dared not allow his mother, who doted on the Crenshaw's daughter, false hope nor any excuse at all whatsoever to clap her hands.

"And the fair Miss Crenshaw?" Lord Avery asked as he led his son into the drawing room, utterly dashing his son's hopes of a quiet evening. "Was she happy to see you after so long? What am I saying? Of course she must have been! There isn't a finer young gentleman in the realm," he claimed as he poured out a drink and pushed a glass into Harry's hand.

He took the glass and smiled in spite of the ringing in his ears that followed each of his father's pronouncements, relieved that he needn't bother with his 'Bertie' masquerade whilst in his parent's presence. They could not possibly see him in any light other than the one of their making; in their eyes, he was perfect, polished, and incapable of taking any action they had not first dreamed up in his behalf. Their blind worship of this extension of themselves had landed him neatly over more than one patch of rough ground growing up and had caused a scandalous number of household servants to throw up their hands and quit the premises altogether.

"Father, I thank you for your confidence in me," he said as he took a sip of his drink whilst shooting a discreet glance over at his mother to gauge her reaction, "though I believe it has been bruited about as to how Miss Crenshaw is promised to her cousin." Since his arrival home, he had longed for the right moment to broach this very subject and had accepted the assignment to return to England expressly for the opportunity to intervene if the rumor were true. He felt prepared for anything but when his mother matter-of-factly confirmed its veracity, he felt the blood in his veins turn to ice.

"Oh, yes!" Lady Avery said so emphatically the pins that fastened her lace cap to her still-golden hair came loose from their moorings. "It has been decided in the mind of his father, the old Duke, this age. However," she said with a fervent clap, "we all know Miss Crenshaw has eyes for none but you, *mon petit*!"

Harry wished to make light of his mother's response, but his mouth had gone so dry, speech was impossible. To keep Mira tethered to his side would be difficult enough without her impending debut in London, but this verification of a *de facto* betrothal was the heaviest of blows. He set down his glass with care so as to disguise the shaking of his hand and went to the fender by the fire to scrape his boots and regain his composure.

"My son," his father said, placing a heavy hand on Harry's shoulder, "a viscount and future earl of the realm has no cause to doubt his value at the bargaining table, even when pitted against a duke."

Harry felt something more than antipathy towards his father for the first time in years. Brushing the hand from his shoulder, Harry turned to face his parent. "Do you truly believe the Crenshaws care a farthing for a title? That Mira would trade happiness for Marcross?" He could all but feel the sneer on his face and turned away so as not to further alarm his mother. "Besides, Sir Anthony is too kind to force her hand where her heart does not lead."

"I cannot understand why you are so downcast, *mon cher*," Lady Avery said. "I do believe you are correct. Anthony was once promised to *moi,* and though it was only for a day and a night, or perhaps a bit more," she said with a faraway look in her eyes, "he cast me, along with my papa's best-loved wineglasses, ruthlessly aside so as to marry a mere Miss Delacourt."

"That is not precisely what happened," Lord Avery hastened to add.

"But I am sure it was wineglasses he broke! They were the ones with the gilt edging, and if Anthony hadn't already broken the engagement along with my heart, Papa would have insisted I not be allowed to marry him for the sake of those glasses alone!"

Harry felt his father's sigh rather than heard it. "That is neither here nor there, Lucinda," he said in painfully clipped tones. "However, your mother is correct," Lord Avery said somewhat grudgingly, "in that the Crenshaws marry for love. The fact that Sir Anthony's engagement to your mother was nothing but a pretense for reasons I refuse to divulge at the moment," he added with a jerk of his head in his wife's direction, "is but a distraction from the truth—that truth being that Miss Crenshaw, like her father and mother before her, will follow her heart, wineglasses or no."

"Oh, Eustace!" Lady Avery said with a flurry of claps. "I had forgotten for the teensiest moment how splendidly romantic you are! Do you not recall the poem you wrote for me, the one where you went on and on about how much you would love to eat me, hair and all?"

"Yes, my flower," Lord Avery said for what was most likely the one hundredth time that day. Not for the first time, Harry felt for his father a deep pity mingled with something far less familiar: gratitude. Harry reached out to give his father a squeeze on the shoulder and turned his attention to the distraction of his mother long enough for her husband to make his escape into the library—a room calculated to be replete with comfort and cigar smoke, no clapping allowed.

"Mother," Harry said with an enthusiasm successfully feigned through many years of practice, "let's say you and I set up the card table and have a game of whist!"

"I don't believe I should enjoy it much tonight," she said with toss of her head.

"Please, Mama," Harry said as he eased himself onto the sofa next to her. "I am persuaded you shall win this time, every round!"

"Truly?" she asked as she studied him from the corner of her eye.

"Truly!"

"All right, then, let's do!" she said and practically flew to the corner of the room to collect the cards from the green baize table. "Only, we shall stay seated here on the sofa by the fire and have a little coze, just you and I."

Harry, only too glad to leave off the subject of love, engagements, and broken hearts, was happy to comply with any and all of her demands for the time being, even if they grew tiresome and petty. As a result, he was caught off guard when her first question was a very pointed and dangerous one.

"Harry," she said in wheedlesome tone, "if I were to beg you tell me the meaning of the letter that arrived today via special messenger, would you?"

Harry froze. He had never known his mother to be quite so calculating and was thoroughly unprepared for her to question anything that did not directly involve herself. Perhaps 'Bertie' should be required to make an appearance after all. Studying a card as if it were of paramount importance, he hedged his bets. "What would I know about a message for my lord?"

"Oh, was it meant for your father? I am persuaded it was addressed to you."

Harry abandoned his hand, sat back, and studied his mother. She had sounded as guileless as ever, yet it was clear she had something up her sleeve and it wasn't made of pasteboard. "Mother, I believe I have sadly underestimated you."

"Yes, dear, I do believe you have," his mother said as mild as a morning in May.

"If I tell you, you must promise not to breathe a word to anyone!" He was aghast at himself for the indiscretion he contemplated, but he was home and he was lonely and the person he held closest to his heart was further away than ever. "You mustn't even tell my lord father. Are you able to do that?"

"Pshaw!" Lady Avery said with an airy wave of the hand. "Have I not kept secret for all these years that I was once betrothed to Anthony Crenshaw? And how the Duke is forever insisting he is all but engaged to Miss Crenshaw? I haven't said the teensiest, weensiest word about that though I have wanted to desperately!" she said in an anguished voice. "And then there's the fact that Anthony proposed marriage to the Duke's mother. She said no, of course, and married the old Duke, though that was after she married the ancient Earl of Derby. I have known about that, well—oh my!—it seems forever, though I couldn't have been more than three years of age at the time."

Harry felt as if his world had shifted on its axis. Mira's father was once enamored of the widowed wife of the old Duke, his uncle? Could this be why a match between her son and his daughter was in the offing? Could Sir Anthony still have feelings for the Duchess? If so, his impression of a very happy domestic life between he and Lady Crenshaw was largely an illusion of Harry's own making. Worse, what chance might he possibly have of making Mira his wife when her father was in the pocket of someone as powerful as the Duchess of Marcross?

"Herbert? Herbert! Are you not listening?" Lady Avery urged. "You haven't told me about the secret letter. Not one word! And I have been waiting for what seems like weeks!"

"Yes, Mother," Harry said with a practiced smile. "And you are correct, you are a most worthy keeper of secrets. Only, this is more serious than who is to marry whom. People are likely to, well, not to put too fine a point on it, *die* if you were to share what I am about to tell you."

Harry was gratified to see how large her eyes had grown, but was still not satisfied she would not betray his trust. "The one most likely to die should you divulge my secret is myself . . . or the Queen."

"The Queen!" his mother cried. "Who cares a pin for the likes of that German woman? The reigning king or queen of England should possess French ancestry, as do we, the Havershams."

"Doubtless many a French sovereign has felt the same," Harry mused, denying himself the impulse to correct his mother as to the origin of their exceedingly English surname. "That is, in fact, the very crux of the matter."

Lady Avery gasped and covered her mouth with her fingers. "They want you to marry the young Queen! How terribly exciting! But how that should kill either of you, I couldn't say," she said with a little shake of her head.

"No, Mother, neither could I," Harry said, shifting in his seat. "Of course I am not to marry Queen Victoria. As French as some of my ancestors might possibly have been, I am not of the Blood Royal. More to the point, there are those who feel that our beloved Queen is not the monarch they would have seated upon England's throne."

"Now you are twitting me, Herbert!" Lady Avery said with a moue. "I can't see how Noah has a thing to do with Queen Victoria, German or no."

Harry stifled a sigh then took heart in the thought that should his mother ever divulge his secret, she would be hard pressed to find anyone who understood her, let alone believe her. "Not '*mon* ark.' 'Monarch', as in, the ruler on the throne."

"Oh! Well then, we are back to that German woman."

Harry let loose his first laugh of pleasure in what seemed like years. "Mother, you are a true original. I think perhaps that is enough for tonight, but if further letters arrive for me, special delivery or no, I shall need to see them immediately and without Father learning about them. Can you do that?"

"*Mais, oui*!" Lady Avery said with a Gallic shrug of her shoulders. "Anything to get a proper French woman on the throne of England!"

With a wince, Harry scratched his head and thought carefully before he spoke. "I am persuaded you would prefer it if Queen Victoria were not foully murdered. Should I not answer the call to be in her service to protect her?"

"Of course!" Lady Avery exclaimed, rising from her seat. "If this is what makes you happy, *mon coeur,*" she added and gave him a peck on the cheek. "Now I am off to *mon chamber* to await your *papa,*" she announced, which prompted another wince from her son who remained, staring into the fire.

It was true that the information he was entrusted to obtain made him responsible for the Queen's health and happiness. Yet, he was responsible for his own as well. And what of Mira's? She could never be happy married to the Duke. Not that Mira wouldn't make a fine duchess; she possessed beauty, intelligence, charm and strength of character, all virtues that would serve her well as George's wife. They would also serve Harry well as his viscountess, and what's more, she loved him. At least he believed she had, once upon a time.

How to woo his maiden fair without exposing his secret? On the one hand, his 'Bertie' act would immediately discount him as the person the Queen's enemies even now hunted. On the other hand, he could hardly win Mira's love as the flibbertigibbet Bertie. He sighed again and raked his fingers through his golden hair. Being an adult was deuced difficult in spite of the fact he had never had the luxury of being otherwise, not in the home of the childlike Lady Avery and her childish lord.

What he would have given for just one barefooted run through the lake at the bottom of the Abbey garden; or a climb up a tree without his mother chiding him for shredding his satin breeches; or a crack at holding the reins of his own pony and trap, a gift from his mother who thought he would look *tres adorable* seated in it but was never allowed to actually drive.

If it hadn't been for his romps through the parks and gardens at Prospero Park with Mira and her brothers, he would have grown up a very odd man indeed. It was Sir Anthony who taught him how to ride, how to shoot and hunt, how to skin a rabbit and fish with a pole. The day eventually arrived when Harry's father felt him old enough to mount a horse and was surprised to find his son already an enviable horseman. Lord Avery was so pleased with his son's prowess, he persuaded Lady Avery to allow it. Once the first hurdle was crossed, his parents delighted in his accomplishments as if it were they themselves who had taught him all.

His years abroad had deepened his skills and added new ones, such as archery, fencing, and even a smattering of sailing. Latin and French, as well as the many ways and means one arrived at one's destination undetected, were subjects of which he was already master. Italian, Greek, and German soon followed. The combination of his physical, intellectual, and survival skills, along with his natural allegiance to the country of his birth, made him the perfect choice for a secret serviceman for the young Queen of England.

Herbert, Viscount Haversham, was an adult—one with responsibilities, commitments, and a job to doone who had left the letter from Lord Melbourne's secretary waiting too long. With the last indulgent sigh Harry would allow himself that night, he got to his feet and went to work.

chapter three

Mira felt dinner to have lasted a lifetime already, and there was still the fruit and cheese course to get through. As dinner was served early in the country, there was still the long evening to be tolerated before she could get into bed and close her eyes on, this, the last day before her debutante Season in London. Her trunks were packed, her traveling costume laid out in anticipation, and she and Mama and Papa would depart at first light with her brothers to follow as it suited.

Of course, much of her clothing would be selected and done up in London, but none could possibly find fault with the new wardrobe she and her mother had ordered at the local drapery shop. As such, they would do until she could have a few more ball gowns, walking dresses, a riding habit, and her court dress bespoken from Wembley House, the townhouse her father had inherited from the old Duchess, his grandmother.

In the meantime, the most exciting thing likely to happen was if one of the servants suddenly broke out in spots. With a sigh, she gazed about the room for conversational inspiration but found none. Perhaps this was as good a time as any to bring up the question she had been burning to ask since Harry's visit to Prospero Park a few days prior.

"Mama," she asked in as bland a tone of voice as she could muster so as not to alert anyone to her rather inappropriate question. "Why did Harry not come home after Eton? Is it not strange that he should embark on a voyage across the ocean for so many months without first returning home to see his parents?" The words *and me* were thought but not spoken.

"Nothing strange about that, in my opinion," Stephen replied. "I daresay you would get as far away as you could, as fast as you could, and for as long as possible if you had that pair waiting for you at the Abbey."

Lady Crenshaw bent a look of disapproval on her older son then turned her attention to her daughter. "I do believe it had something to do with his parents, but not what your brother suggests. Harry has always been a devoted son in spite of his father's demanding nature."

"I always found his father to be somewhat tolerable," Adrian commented, "but his mother . . ." he added with a shake of his head as if mere words failed him, an action that prompted a bark of laughter from his father, one that was quickly followed by a fit of feigned coughing into his monogrammed napkin.

"Anthony, you know it won't do to encourage the boys in their vilification of Lord and Lady Avery," Lady Crenshaw reprimanded. "As I have said on numerous occasions," she outlined for the benefit of the entire family, "they are not precisely our friends as we are quite beneath them socially. However, they are our neighbors, as well as Harry's parents, so it would not do to treat them other than with the dignity called for by their position."

"I believe it to have been Harry we were discussing in the first place," Mira said, her words sounding lofty in her own ears. Surely it would not do to come across as quite so dramatic once she arrived in London, and she was determined to gain some refinement sooner rather than later. "Mama, at the time you said his departure for Europe straight from school had something to do with Lord and Lady Avery. What might that have been?" she asked, congratulating herself on her staid delivery.

"I believe it was nothing more than his mama's fancy that he should be exposed to as much of the French culture as soon as possible," her mother replied.

"It doesn't seem to have done him much good," Stephen said with a scowl. "I preferred him as he was before he put on his Frenchified airs. Besides which, I had always thought it had most to do with that rowing accident."

Mira was aware of a speaking look her mother gave her father who cleared his throat and made his foray into the conversation. "The rowing accident was just that; an accident. Meanwhile, your mother is quite correct when she says that we mustn't belittle Harry or his parents, though I must own I have a very low opinion of his new attitude."

With an exasperated smile, Lady Crenshaw put down her goblet with a decided thump against the tabletop. "Anthony, you know that is not the remonstration I had in mind."

"I realize that, dear, but it was the one *I* had in mind, and quite literally, I might add."

The gales of laughter that followed her father's remark seemed more than a little brash. Her brothers were two and three years older than she, but they often behaved as if they were mere children. It was enough to convince her that she ought to look for an older man among the claimants for her hand at the end of the Season. Mira could not fathom why Harry's face should flash into her mind with the thought, as 'Bertie' had turned out to be the most childish of all the boys with whom she had grown up. Idly, she wondered if he might be different if he had not gone to the Continent straight from Eton, but she dismissed the idea almost as quickly as she thought it. Harry was of an age with Stephen, and there was no question *he* was too young to contemplate marriage in the near future, Grand Tour or no.

Later that evening, as she stitched new ribbons into her periwinkle blue calash, Mira thought again of Harry; not the Harry she once knew and certainly not 'Bertie,' but the Harry who had looked at her with such intensity when he had visited Prospero Park only a few days prior. For that one moment, there was something about the expression in his eyes that made her heart feel a bit wrenched whenever the memory came to mind. It was as if the man that stood before her for that sliver in time was altogether a different person from the youthful Harry she once knew and the childish version she did not recognize.

This ephemeral Harry was far too taciturn for her taste, but he was also ardent, manly, and entirely present. In the intervening days since they met, she had spent a fair amount of time in imaginary conversation with him, and the thought had occurred to her that it should prove difficult to find a suitor to compare with the very real Harry she had invented in her mind.

Her Harry was an excellent conversationalist, wiser than his years, filled out his tasteful clothing to admiration, treated a girl like a lady, and, just for good measure, was capable of banishing danger with a flick of his finger. She supposed it was a dash dramatic, but, in case it were necessary, he was fully capable of wrestling a tiger or two. Lastly, but far from least important, one look from him would cause her stomach to flutter in much the same fashion it had a few days previous. In fact, it fluttered still every time she thought of the way his green gaze clung to her own.

Suddenly, fresh ribbons for her headgear for the trip to London seemed utterly superfluous unless Harry were to see her with the very bow tied under her chin. Her new cape of bottle green she had been in raptures over only the week before seemed insignificant, nay, downright insipid if Harry were not to see how it brought out the sheen in her red curls. Even the most recent addition to her wardrobe, kid leather boots with tiny rosettes, seemed dull as ditch water unless they made Harry's eyes shine.

How lamentable that Harry was a figment of her imagination. There was only 'Bertie,' and she hadn't the slightest desire to be admired by him, now or ever. She felt much the same about her cousin, George, who, as the Duke of Marcross, must be addressed by his title in spite of the fact that as children she had seen him with jam smeared all over his face on more than a few occasions. The Duke, however, was not as easily avoided most especially since he, without warning, joined Mira and her parents on their journey to London the following morning. It was all she could do not to cry out in dismay when he cantered up to the house as the family boarded their carriage.

"My dearest Miss Crenshaw, I am enchanted," he said as he swung down from his seat.

She suppressed a shudder and gave him her hand to kiss with hopes his mouth would reach her skin prior to the exceedingly sharp tip of his nose—a sentiment of which she immediately repented when his warm, moist lips found their quarry.

"George, ah, I mean to say Your Grace, how fortunate we are that you are to accompany us on our journey," Mira said. The gratified look on her mother's face did not escape her and caused Mira to suspect that this particular meeting was one Lady Crenshaw had known of for some time.

"Yes, your esteemed father agreed, upon receipt of my missive suggesting it, that it would be best if I saw you safely to your destination. Sir Anthony, my good man," George added, turning to her father with a hearty shake of his cousin's hand, recalling to Mira's mind that her father was, since the death of her great-uncle, heir to the present Duke. Being that George was of an age with her elder brother, she wondered how her father tolerated being treated in such a superior fashion and fancied that she detected a shadow cross his face.

"Shall we be off then?" Lady Crenshaw suggested with an arch look for her husband. The fact that she was miffed by George's failure to greet her was evident in her expression. His decided prejudice against Lady Crenshaw's inadequate pedigree was one of the reasons Mira despised him so. She suspected the matter, to her mother, didn't much signify, but Mira had reason to believe she had other reasons for disliking George. Though she wasn't precisely sure what her mother's reasons were specifically, there were plenty from which to choose.

She suppressed another shudder as her cousin handed her into the carriage and settled into the velvet squabs, relieved that George would be taking most of the journey via horseback. As always, she chose to be seated next to her father, in part to have the chance to be near him, but also to witness how her mother's expression softened as Sir Anthony went through the ritual of asking if his wife was quite comfortable and if there were anything she needed. Only then and not before would he take his own seat across from her, whereupon he would lean back, his hat low on his brow so as to cover his eyes, and would at once fall asleep.

It hadn't taken Mira long to determine her father was merely feigning slumber since her mother's soft chuckle would immediately rouse her father who would then, more often than not, reach across the carriage to take his wife's hand and give it a gentle squeeze. It was then, and only then that he would turn to Mira to ensure that she was properly settled as well. Mira had asked both of her parents on various occasions what it all meant, but their reply of "It's just a little joke of Grandmama's from years ago," was not terribly illuminating.

One day she would draw the full story from their lips, but for now she watched the ritual play out with enjoyment as she dreamed about a husband of her own with whom she would share secret smiles. It was not surprising in the least that her imaginary Harry should come to mind with the thought since the single glimpse she had of him was one in which his eyes had spoken volumes. Perhaps someday she would have the courage to draw the full story of that speaking glance from his lips as well, and she shivered with delight at the prospect.

Though they planned to suspend their travel at the halfway point to spend the night in an inn, the journey to London from Prospero Park took only the better part of a day.

However, it was clear from the comments her parents made each and every time they made it that it had been a longer one in their time. As always, the discussion in the carriage revolved around how much improved the roads were, how much smoother the carriages were these days, and how swifter the exchange at the toll booths. There was also the usual talk with regards to how many estates had sprung up along the way, as well as how many more coaching inns, pubs, and shops, and so on and so forth until Mira thought she might scream. Screams, however, would not be well received, and she was a young lady on the brink of presentation to the Queen. Surely there was a better way to draw her parents' attention to the fact that she was near to expired with boredom.

"Mama, is George to stay with us or will he have Crenshaw House opened for his use?"

Lady Crenshaw sighed and gripped her hands together more tightly in her lap. "I believe we'll find that his mother has arrived ahead of us. Surely she will be taking up residence at Crenshaw House and will no doubt insist upon George joining her."

Mira watched with fascination as her mother's hands relaxed with naught but a gentle nudge of her father's foot against his lady's slipper. It was if there were some secret language they were speaking. Taking up her fan, she hid her smile behind it before returning her attention once again to her daughter. "George is family and a very nice young man, but I am just as glad he will be staying in his own house. Besides, 'tis easier to always look your best for your beau when he is not underfoot, is it not?"

Mira was sure she didn't know, never having had any beaux, underfoot or otherwise. However, that was neither here nor there when one contemplated the enormity of her mother's implication. "Surely," she said, turning to her father for support, "I should expect more than George to call on me, should I not?"

"Of course you should, sweetheart!" her father said, patting her hand. "I have no doubt there shall be dozens of gentleman callers and even more invitations to any manner of social gatherings. Wasn't it the same for you the year you made your bows, my love?" he added for the benefit of his wife.

"I would remind you not to make me a figure of fun if you please, sir," Lady Crenshaw said with a snap of her fan. "You know very well that I didn't take well, and if it were not for you, I should be firmly on the shelf, even now."

Mira laughed at what she could only assume was a jest. To her dismay, she laughed alone. "No!" she cried. "You can't be serious. Mother, you are so beautiful! How can you not have been the belle of every ball?"

"She was the belle of every ball I attended," her father said with an intent gaze for his wife. Hastily, he cleared his throat and said, "Wasn't it just the other day you were commenting on the dowdy fashions of eighteen-twelve? So, there you have it! I must have been one of the few gentlemen capable of seeing past her abominable bonnets."

With a laugh of delight, Lady Crenshaw turned her attention to the view out the window.

"You said 'few gentlemen,' Papa. Surely you weren't the only suitor who begged for her hand in marriage, wretched bonnets or no," Mira quizzed.

"To be sure, I wasn't! But that must be your mother's story to tell in her own time."

Mira looked to her mother for further enlightenment, but she merely smiled and continued to watch the landscape fly past the carriage window.

"Am I not to know? How is a young lady to learn from her mother's triumphs and despairs without the proper information?" Mira demanded.

"Miranda," Lady Crenshaw said, leaning forward with a rustling of skirts to take her daughter's hands in her own. "You are cut from a very specific bolt of cloth, to be sure. Never fear, my dear. Unlike myself who had no mother or father to advise me or lend me countenance, you have one of each to guide you. Besides, there is always George, especially if Harry continues to behave so unbecomingly in the drawing rooms of London. You shall not be long on the Marriage Mart, my girl," she insisted, giving Mira's hands a squeeze.

Mira pulled free from her mother's grasp and allowed her hands to drop to her lap. The wave of horror that overcame her whenever she thought of her parents' baffling willingness to fall in with the plans of George's father was quickly followed by a new sensation: anger. She loved her parents dearly and knew they only wanted what was best for her and could never be angry with *them.* No, her anger was for Harry, who had allowed himself to become a fop and a dandy. What had happened to the young man with whom she had enjoyed swimming, riding, and shooting? Certainly 'Bertie' wouldn't dream of engaging in any of those activities. How could he possibly with so much lace dripping from his wrists?

As she turned her own attention to the landscape outside, Mira mused on what might have happened to Harry to turn him into such a travesty. It clearly occurred whilst he was away, so perhaps something had happened to him either at Eton or on the Continent. Since her brothers attended Harrow, there was no guarantee they would know how much responsibility could be laid at the door of Eton in particular, and since they were still very much the same boys they had been prior to boarding school, she decided boarding school in general could not be the problem.

George was an *alma mater* of Eton as well, and as he was precisely the same creature he had been prior to his years there, it most likely had nothing to do with the school in particular. She supposed she might ask George about the rowing accident since it was clear her parents had said all they would on the subject. However, she must first weigh it all out in her mind so as not to lead George to believe her interest in Harry was anything but perfectly idle. Being that her interest was far from it, this could prove difficult to accomplish. At the same time, were she to approach him with a question of any kind, he would doubtless take it as a token of esteem, and she had no wish to encourage George in the slightest degree.

Finally, she threw up her hands in exasperation, startling her genuinely slumbering father out of somnolence, before she gave her thoughts over to the far less demanding task of mentally choosing the fabric to be made into her court gown. She owned that it was a bit hypocritical of her when she had been so hard on 'Bertie' and his fussy ensemble, but surely a woman was allowed more contemplation of clothing than the stronger sex. Besides, if both man and wife were entirely caught up in their wardrobes, they would soon be bankrupt. Thank goodness Mama did not feel the need for dozens of gowns or there would be little left in the coffers for Mira's clothes once Papa had made his usual inroads. At least he eschewed lace at his cuffs . . . mostly.

Mira hadn't time to dwell much longer on her attire for there came a knock on the window glass. Mira opened the window, and George made it known that the carriage would any moment be coming to a halt at the next establishment so as to take refreshment.

"Look there, my darling," her father said as he gazed out the window. "It is not called the same yet it is . . . yes! The very same inn!"

"What inn is that?" Mira asked.

"Oh, it is merely an establishment at which your father and I partook of a meal on a very memorable occasion. I do hope they have since improved the place," Lady Crenshaw said, misgiving lining her face.

As Mira wondered what defined a 'memorable occasion,' the carriage pulled into the yard, and the steps were let down. She was startled when it was her turn to disembark, and George offered her his arm, insisting she take it for the journey across the yard and through the front door of The Cygnet and Lute.

"You must familiarize yourself to my ways, Miss Crenshaw," he said with an oily smile. "It would not do for the Duchess of Marcross to take herself through the door when I am at her disposal."

It was with great reluctance that Mira took his arm. "I fail to see what your mother has to do with it as she is not present," Mira said with a toss of her head.

"Oh, but there you are wrong, my dear. I could hardly speak before you make your bows to the queen, but it is common knowledge that you shall be the next Duchess of Marcross. Certainly your devoted parents have shared with you the news of our impending nuptials. I am persuaded they are as delighted as I am at the prospect. What could be more fortuitous than to have the daughter of my father's former heir secure the title that should have been her mother's?"

Indignant, Mira pulled her hand from his arm in time to prevent it being clamped tightly to his side. "I am persuaded Mother mourned not the loss, George," she said with a humiliating emphasis on his given name. "As for my father, he would have doubtless carried his title with distinction in spite of never having expected the honor. I have heard it said that the old Duke's first son, the one who died so long ago, was very much loved by one and all. I am sorry he is not here to enjoy what should have been his." And with that she pushed past George into The Cygnet and Lute.

chapter four

Harry watched in consternation as the Crenshaw party descended upon the very taproom he had chosen in which to break his journey over a shepherd's pie and a tankard of ale. For the ale he was most particularly grateful as it was sorely needed to wash down the dinner lodged against the sudden lump that formed in his throat upon the sight of Miss Crenshaw. His anxiety over her welfare, as well as that of her parents, could not be as easily assuaged; there were those who wanted Harry dead for the knowledge he possessed, and he had been shot at only that morning as he had made his way via horseback to meet his secret service contact at the inn. Harry hoped the inn too public a place for a gunman to make another attempt; if not, anyone in Harry's orbit was in danger of suffering a similar fate. Should his enemies learn of Harry's attachment to Mira in particular, they would not hesitate to use her any way they chose as a means of coercing Harry to divulge his secrets.

Fortunately, Higgins, the gentleman seated across from him, seemed not to notice Harry's sudden discomposure and continued with the low-toned accounting of his orders. Harry learned that when he reached London, he was to take rooms at Claridge's under a fictitious name. Next, he was to await a specific knock on his door at which time he would depart for the Royal Botanic Gardens at Kew. Once arrived, he was to make his way to the top of the Great Pagoda and await further instruction.

Harry wasn't precisely sure he knew where in the gardens the Great Pagoda stood, but his childhood memory of it assured him that it was stupendously tall and impossible to miss. He suspected his climb to the top of the stairs of the nearly eighty-year-old edifice would prove to be amongst his most dangerous assignments, though not nearly as dangerous as the line Harry just heard George cross during the course of his current conversation with Miss Crenshaw. George was Mira's cousin and very possibly her intended husband, but Harry would not sit still while George behaved like a lecher set loose in a harem.

Harry wiped his mouth with his napkin, tossed it to the table, and sauntered across the room to the Crenshaw party, remembering just in time to add the appropriate mince to his step. Though he would much rather have charged ahead to greet the top-lofty Duke with a fist to the chin, he forced himself to go slowly and use the intervening moments to envelope himself in the 'Bertie' façade.

"La, what do we have here?" he asked when he could trust his voice to sound free of fury. "Why, it's Marcross!" For more than one reason he ignored George's out-thrust hand and opted to tap the arrogant young nobleman's shoulder instead. "I do believe, yes I *do* believe it has been since Eton that we have met!"

George was stunned into silence while the Crenshaws exchanged a speaking glance. It was a sudden stroke of inspiration that prompted Harry to adopt his Grandfather Barrington's conversational cadences, and it would seem from the expressions on their faces that the Crenshaws had most certainly met the old Squire. As no response was forthcoming, Harry cast about for a way to keep the conversation alive. A fruitful idea would be to address his comments to Mira, but that could prove dangerous as well; he knew his longing for one word of love, friendship, or even approval from her would be far too apparent, if not positively naked.

Turning his back on his beloved, he addressed her mother instead. "Lady Crenshaw, I declare, I heard a droll joke the other day. A *bon mot tres amusant*, if I do say so myself." He followed this up with an obnoxious laugh in spite of the way the thundering of his heart impinged on his capacity to fill his lungs for he suddenly had the most lively sense of danger. The thought that his presence alone might put Mira and her parents in peril caused the muscles in his stomach to clench, and he swept a gaze about the room before pausing to look again on Lady Crenshaw's curiosity-filled face.

"Har . . . Bertie, pray tell," she said with an indulgent smile, "what is this *tres bon mot*?"

He realized with sudden horror that few of the jokes to which he had been exposed over the years were appropriate for the gentler sex. If he didn't come up with something foolish and frivolous on the spot, his behavior would seem very suspicious indeed. Anxious to ensure Mira's safety from unseen forces, he could not resist turning to face her. The expression in her eyes made him just as anxious to hide from her perceptive gaze; hastily dropping his own, he stared fixedly at the fan she held in her hand upon which inspiration lighted.

"Why does the fan not like the lute?" he asked, unable to hold back a genuine smile of relief.

"I couldn't say," the Duke drawled in blatant imitation of Harry. He did not smile.

"Because it's not a fan of instruments!" Harry exclaimed, tacking on another round of obnoxious laughter in an attempt to distract all and sundry from dwelling overly long on the utter absurdity of his attempt at humor. George's predictable negative reaction notwithstanding, Harry was humbled and more than a little pleased at the kindness of the Crenshaw family, all of whom managed a chuckle and smile of encouragement. From her parents he would have expected nothing less, but for Mira to favor him with something as benevolent as a smile at an utterly inane joke uttered by an equally inane man was a gift indeed. Perhaps there was hope for 'Bertie' after all.

With a cough to conceal his crow of delight, Harry turned away from the Crenshaws and came face-to-face with Higgins whose severe expression and rigid stance implied the reality of the peril Harry had sensed earlier.

"That was a right funny ditty," Higgins said with a barely perceptible jerk of his head towards the entrance.

"I'm to be damned by faint praise, am I?" Harry murmured with a cock of his brow and another visual sweep of the room that revealed nothing untoward.

"You're sure to be some kind of damned if we don't scarper out of here," Higgins said under his breath.

"Right!" Harry said, clapping his arm about Higgins shoulders and pivoting the two of them about to address the Crenshaws. "Your Grace, Sir Anthony, Lady Crenshaw, Miss Crenshaw," he said with a nod of his head for each. "Sadly, I must bid you *adieu*! It seems, yes it *seems*, I am meant to be elsewhere!" he twittered. "Until London," he added with a last veiled glimpse of Mira from the corner of his eye.

"Nitwit," George muttered as he placed his well-shod foot directly in the path of the now-hastening Harry who was sent sprawling to the floor just as a loud crack split the air and general pandemonium ensued. Harry recovered quickly and rolled under the table to come to rest against Mira's feet, fetchingly encased in kid boots he noticed to be covered in the sweetest ribbon roses. Before he could formulate a plan, the owner of the boots lowered her face, pale and wide-eyed, beneath the table.

"Harry! What is happening?" she asked in a harsh whisper, the sound of sobs and screaming a crazed din in the background.

With her fear-filled face so close to his own, Harry was bereft of thought. His wants were in command of his actions, and what he wanted was to keep her safe. What he longed for, and had for quite some time, was to have her close. Rising to a crouch, he took the hand that held aloft the tablecloth and tugged her down to the floor at his side. She opened her mouth to say he knew not what, for he quickly hushed her so as to better determine the state of affairs beyond the confines of the table legs. He heard Sir Anthony tell his wife to get down, then commend the safekeeping of his women folk to, of all people, the now hysterical George who called out to his cousin not to leave him. If there were a more useless article in the room, it would have to be Higgins, whom, he assumed, had taken a bullet. Harry fervently hoped Higgins had made his escape, but either way, Harry was on his own.

"Harry!" Mira cried. She rose to her knees to face him, and he became suddenly aware that the thundering of his heart was not from fear but brought on by the proximity of the redheaded beauty at his side whose gaze, even now, met his in a frankly disconcerting way. The danger that awaited him beyond the tablecloth was nothing compared to the danger beneath, and his face burned with the turn his thoughts had taken.

Yet, he could not deny the pure beauty of his situation. Their position afforded them a privacy he might never again know in her presence. He would not forgive himself if he did not take advantage of what could be his only opportunity to demonstrate his yearning. Finally, tormented by conflicting desires, he threw caution to the wind and kissed her full on her bow-shaped mouth.

Harry wasn't sure if the ringing in his ears had been as loud the last time she had slapped him; her petite hand couldn't have been much smaller when he had kissed her in days of old. However, it definitely pained him more this time, of that he was certain.

"Why, Harry Haversham, you haven't changed a bit!"

Alarmed by the way the curve of her lips belied the smolder in her eyes, Harry delayed his response. He narrowed his gaze upon her and fell to pondering the solutions to a number of difficulties: how to gracefully extricate himself from his hidey-hole without getting shot; how to get a heavily blushing Mira from under the table without anyone guessing what had transpired; and how to convince the love of his life that he was a mere fop and a fribble without forever putting paid to his intended role as the love of hers, each of which had to be accomplished in a trice or all was lost.

"Pray, I do say, *pray* forgive me, Miss Crenshaw!" Harry squeaked. "I suppose I must have got caught up in the moment. I thought perhaps I was to die this very moment, and as I have never kissed a girl . . ."

"Never?" Mira sputtered.

Hiding a coy smile behind his fingers, Harry thought furiously, mentally mapping out the location of Marcross, who must never know anything of what had just happened at his feet; Sir Anthony, who was Harry's best hope for an ally, but who Harry presumed had gone in pursuit of the shooter; Lady Crenshaw, who was even now beginning to lift the tablecloth from the far side of the table; and his would-be assailant who could be just about anywhere, all of which were paltry concerns compared to producing a suitable reply to Mira's challenge.

"Uh, well . . . Oh! Was that *you?*" Harry asked, his eyes wide with innocence all the while feeling himself the vilest of creatures, the kind who could forget kissing such a girl as Mira, young as she had been at the time, or worse, lie about it. With a mental wince, he plunged on. "I hadn't remembered, no, not remembered it was *you.*"

Mira glared at him and clearly would have stamped her well-shod, little foot were it possible to stand. "You know very well it was me! The possibility that there haven't been any others is highly questionable and, rest assured, I have questions. Meanwhile, Harry or Bertie or whoever you are, something dubious, impugnable and indeterminate is going on, not to mention crepuscular and downright hazy, and I intend to put my faculties to their utmost in discovering what it is that you are hiding!"

"I should not if I were you," Harry said in an ice-cold voice he barely recognized as his own. He had heard it said there are times when one must be cruel to be kind, but he never believed it until this moment. "I suggest you tend to your mother before she finds it necessary to join us, then drag the caterwauling George to safety, followed by your complete and utter forgetfulness of all that has occurred in this accursed inn."

"I suppose this means you intend to forget that you kissed me under one of the tables of said inn, as well as the fact that you, sir, are nothing but a liar," Mira hissed.

Harry was persuaded no collection case butterfly could possibly feel as skewered as he. Time and circumstances, however, did not allow for explanations. To turn away from Mira's anguished, sapphire-blue eyes framed by glossy ringlets he longed to touch was doubtless the most difficult thing he might ever hope to do—but do it he must. Without a word, he ducked his head between his shoulders, crawled from beneath the table, and nimbly under the next as quickly as limbs, both of wood and flesh, would allow.

As luck would have it, the supply of tables did not run out before he gained the back door to the yard where he was vastly relieved to find Higgins, shot and bleeding but alive, in close consultation with Mira's father. Harry was touched to see the pleasure in Sir Anthony's eyes when he spotted Harry, a sentiment that vanished the moment the vacuous expression of Bertie filled his face.

"Oh, my friends, my friends, how happy I am to see you!" Harry cried as, gingerly, he made his way between one mound of steaming muck after the other. He felt confident that riding boots were created to withstand animal excrement, but suspected Bertie was strongly opposed to anything odiferous hanging about his personage. "I feared I should never see either of you again!" He pulled a handkerchief from his pocket to dab his non-existent tears, surprised to see that his hand shook ever so slightly. Apparently, the shock to his nerves was greater than he supposed, but not anywhere near as great as they must have been to Bertie's. He resisted the urge to quell the shaking and embraced each man in turn with a cry of surprise at sight of Higgins' injured arm, whereupon he proceeded to make a dreadful fuss over it. "Whatever, I say, what*ever* are you to do about that, my dear man?" he wailed as if he hadn't applied his share of tourniquets over the years.

"Tis but a scratch, my lord," Higgins replied in a grave voice. "I am far more concerned about the hare brain who opened fire and where he's got to."

"Yes," Sir Anthony mused, "it was quite shocking, though it should not have been terribly surprising in light of certain nefarious circumstances I have experienced in connection with this particular coaching house," he said, his expression wry. "I spotted the shooter running from the room and went after him. He must have had a mount waiting close by for he was gone by the time I had made it out the door." He clapped a hand to Harry's shoulder and added, "You disappeared so fast, I thought perhaps you had been hit and collapsed under a table somewhere."

"Hit?" Harry squealed. "I? But where?" he demanded, though his alarm had more to do with assignations under tables than with gunfire. "Higgins, do you see any bullet holes?" he asked, and twisted this way and that to inspect his person for damage, including the lace at his wrists about which he couldn't care less, all the while watching Sir

Anthony out of the corner of his eye to gauge his reaction. Was the Bertie act fooling him? And if it were, did a vestige of hope of being given Mira Crenshaw's hand in marriage remain?

"Harry . . ." Sir Anthony said, but was silenced by Harry's wagging finger in his nose. "But of course, it's Bertie now. I don't know if I shall ever grow used to calling you such! Meanwhile, I must find my wife and daughter and make sure they are well. Will you join us back at the inn?"

"I mustn't, no, I mustn't take up any more of your time," Harry averred, "but you may rest assured your lady wife and daughter are in good hands. But wait!" he said, once again snapping his forefinger to attention. Wasn't it the Duke of Marcross with whom they tarried? As such, I must recant," he said with a woeful wag of his head. "The last I saw of him, he was drying his tears with the tablecloth."

"Then I had best hurry. Do be careful, Bertie," Sir Anthony said and disappeared into the inn.

"Well, that Bertie of your'n is a right fine ninny, ain't he?" Higgins said with a snort.

"Aye," Harry agreed, "but there be worse men about."

"No doubt you're referring to that traitor with the pistol."

"None at all," Harry replied while privately wondering if an honest nincompoop such as Bertie weren't a better man than the snide hypocrite Harry was becoming. "Let us part here, you to find a surgeon for that arm and me to track down the gunman," he insisted.

"Nay, 'tis a cold trail already," Higgins said. "I would as lief have you tuck yourself into bed for the remains of the day and continue your journey at night. You'd make a sight less easy target under a moonless sky."

"Doubtless true," Harry agreed. He scanned the horizon for any clue as to the identity of the person who wanted them dead. "I should be a bit of a babe in the woods remaining here though, shouldn't I?"

"Rubbish! This is the last place he'll look. He must know you are headed to London and doubtless has gone ahead to try his luck there. Snug as a rug you'll be here, Harry, mark my words."

"To tell the truth, I would rather feel the muzzle of a gun in my back than take a scolding in the face," Harry said with a rueful smile.

"Eh?"

"Forget I spoke." Harry thrust out his hand to bid Higgins farewell and watched his secret service contact ride out of sight before he reluctantly entered the inn. There was the small matter of having refused to return to the inn with Sir Anthony just a few moments past, while the matter of having kissed his daughter under the table was no small matter indeed. The possibility that Lady Crenshaw witnessed any or all of his and Mira's *tete-a-tete* filled him with a hot and painful dread. He couldn't bear the thought of Lady Crenshaw's displeasure in word or deed. Returning to the inn was the last thing he wanted to do, but Higgins was right; it would be best to cool his heels until nightfall.

Meanwhile, his time would be best spent in the spreading of false rumors as to the nature of the bedlam let loose at the Cygnet and Lute. It simply wouldn't do for a personage such as the Duke of Marcross to bandy it about that someone had been gunning for Harry. A plausible explanation for the gunfire must be thought of, and the malignant expression on George's face when Harry strode into the dining room was all the inspiration he needed.

"Bertie!" Sir Anthony said with some surprise. "I thought you were off already."

"I meant to be, but I felt duty bound to inform you that the Duke's life is in danger," Harry said with a studious determination to avoid Mira's gaze, a task made more difficult when the sound of her gasp met his ears.

George said nothing in reply, but it was clear to Harry that the Duke's overblown ego made it entirely possible for him to swallow such a preposterous notion.

Sir Anthony was not as easily flummoxed, however. "But I'm persuaded the bullet was meant for you. It came close enough to part your hair!"

"Oh, I do hope the bullet was not intended for you, Bertie!" Lady Crenshaw said, upon which a mortified silence fell over the group.

Harry was absurdly grateful for Lady Crenshaw's affectionate response and quickly spoke to cover her lack of concern for the life of the Duke. "Marcross is the most important person in the room. There is no doubt the bullet was intended for him, do you not agree?" he asked with a deferential nod in George's direction whose mulish expression did much to convey his outrage.

"If it were, the gunman was a dashed rotten marksman!"

"Without question," Harry agreed and allowed his glance to fall for a moment on Mira's white face with a surge of gratitude that the gunman did indeed miss. "As a result, I felt it best to offer my services as additional protection," he heard himself say against all reason. It was worth it if it brightened Mira's expression in response.

Apparently the idea appealed to at least one Crenshaw. "I daresay one can never have too many attendants, can one?" George drawled. "Besides, with you riding I am free to travel within the coach," he added with a look for Mira that Harry could not like.

"In that case," Mira said, rising to her feet with a great rustling of skirts, "I suggest we resume our journey in the morning. I have suffered enough abuse for one day, do you not agree, *Bertie*?" she said, her chin a shade higher than normal.

Harry, torn between appreciation for Mira's spirited response to George's lewd behavior and fury at himself for his failure to adequately maintain his Bertie persona, did not trust himself to reply. With a sketch of a bow for each, he followed the hastily retreating Mira from the room.

It was only as he was just about to catch her by the elbow that he remembered his promise to Higgins to sleep by day and travel at night. Yet, as wary as he was of bringing danger down on the heads of those he loved most in the world, he couldn't bear the thought of parting from Mira and leaving her in the clutches of her odious cousin. Somehow he must think of a way to be the beau seated next to her in the traveling coach come morning. More torn in his duty than ever, he remained at the bottom of the stairs watching the red curls bob against the small of Mira's back until she had shut the door of her room behind her.

There was no denying it now; the fat was well and truly in the fire.

chapter five

Mira was persuaded she heard strange sounds during the course of the night. Surely they were mere fancies—the result of having spent the afternoon and evening alone in a small room with naught but her riotous thoughts to keep her company. Unwilling to sup with George, she had bespoken a tray to be sent to her room and retired early but slept ill, fretful over George's self-assured overtures that were hateful in the extreme, especially since he behaved as if their engagement were a decided fact.

As loathsome as was the thought of spending the better part of a day seated next to George in the carriage, Mira felt a deal more vexation over the problem of Harry. The mercurial changes in his character notwithstanding, there was plenty to mull over with regards to his behavior under the dining room table. What could it mean? More importantly, what did she wish it to mean?

She pondered these things as she lolled beneath the bed coverings in the minutes just prior to the rising of the sun but was startled by an echo of the troublesome noises she had heard in the dark of the night. She had thought perhaps it was a rat though it was more of a thumping than a scratching. The possibility of loose shutters and wind-blown branches had all been eliminated long since. When the noise came again, she was able to determine that it originated from the passage outside her door. This ruled out wild animals and other night crawlers and narrowed the choices down to a domestic animal such as a cat, dog, or chicken that had wandered in from the yard under the noses of its betters.

Wildly curious, she slipped out of bed and tiptoed to the door so as not to alert what promised to be a delightful source of relief from her tedium. Quietly, she released the latch and pulled the door open only wide enough to give her a view of the passage floor.

To her great surprise the space was not occupied by an animal of any kind. Rather, a man, as she presumed him to be, stretched along the carpet, his form wrapped entirely in a blanket, might easily be judged an 'animal,' but she felt she should reserve condemnation until she determined the reason for his being where she found him. If he pleaded 'no room at the inn,' she could find it in her heart to excuse his odd behavior. If he were sleeping off a night of riotous drinking and had passed out in front of her room on the way to his own, he was no better than an animal indeed.

"Sir," she whispered so as not to awaken any guests other than the one who had made her threshold his bed. "Sir!" she hissed with a bit more intensity followed by a prod of her slipperless toe to his foot wrapped tight in tartan wool. It was clear that his sense of touch was stronger than that of hearing as this gentle contact brought him to his feet in one catlike leap of his powerful thighs as he dropped the blanket to puddle at his feet. He looked wildly about him, his disordered yellow locks stuck out at odd angles, as his attention finally came to rest on Mira who watched this unexpected spectacle with mouth agape.

"Harry!" she exclaimed whilst privately noting the all too swiftly dampened flare of warmth in his eyes when he saw her. "What are you doing out here? I assume you have your own room?"

"Yes. Yes, I do," he said, looking abashed but not in the mood to further elucidate.

"Lost track of it, have you?" Mira snipped. "Perhaps it's the very same in which you left your boots," she suggested with a pointed look at his shoeless feet.

Harry looked down at the offensive articles then back at Mira with a Bertie-like smile of chagrin. It marred what Mira tended to think of as a masculine face blessed with a strong jaw balanced by striking eyes that were fringed with lashes any woman would envy. His gaze must have followed her thoughts because his eyes rolled upwards, and he clapped his hands to the top of his head just as she arrived at the subject of his hair.

"I must look a devil!" he cried followed by what amounted to a twitter.

Mira wanted nothing more than to roll her eyes as well, but quelled the desire. "I expect the state of your appearance can be rectified through the use of the wash pitcher and mirror made available by the innkeeper. Since these items are generally found in one's room, I suggest you take yourself off forthwith." Besides which, someone could come along the passage at any moment and would no doubt think it odd to find him outside her chamber door in his stockings. After what happened under the table the day prior, Mira felt it best to avoid even a breath of scandal with regards to Harry Haversham.

Unaccountably, he did not go.

"Miss Crenshaw, would it be too much trouble to make use of yours?"

"I'm sorry, I don't understand. Make use of what?"

"Your room," he said with a straightforward intensity that owed nothing to his alter ego, Bertie. "Quickly, now, for a door has just opened up down the passage, one I must pass to arrive at my own."

Without a thought for the impropriety of his request save that of how suddenly similar this Harry was to the one she had been daydreaming about, Mira opened the door just wide enough to allow him to sidle through, whereupon she shut it silently behind him. Once he was in, however, there were few places for him to go. He stood, towering over her as he looked everywhere but at her, a habit of his that had become more than a little distasteful.

Just when she began to worry that her mother would discover them in such a compromising situation, Mira realized he hunted for an alternative exit from the room. It wasn't until he bolted for the window, and she spied the butt of a pistol tucked into the waistband of his breeches that she began to form new opinions as to his continual presence in unexpected locations.

"Harry, are you in some kind of trouble?" she demanded as he thrust one muscular leg through the window. When the other followed and he slid through, she shrieked in alarm, sure he would at any moment completely disappear only to be found dashed to pieces on the ground many feet below. "Harry!" she cried as she dashed to the open casement.

She ought not to have feared for he stood at ease, his feet braced against a piece of molding half a man's length below the window, a hand on each side of the casement, no sign of weakness showing in the muscles that lined his arms. His white shirt fluttered freely in the breeze, as did his hair, and as he leaned into the room, his green eyes blazed with a message she did not fully understand.

Instinctively, she bent towards him, her eyes closed and her lips parted in expectation of a kiss, resolved that, this time, she would not slap him. In fact, should this version of Harry remain, she would never need slap him again. Instead, he put his mouth to her ear to whisper "many thanks." When she opened her eyes, heart pounding in her chest, he was gone.

Yet, he had been there—the Harry of her dreams. The Harry she dreamed of, the man she had always expected him to become, was adventurous, strong, dashing, and brave. Clearly, there was an important reason for him to hide his true self, the one who was startlingly similar to the one she believed herself to have invented, by behaving like a shallow youth. The question, one of many, was whether she were the object of his deceit or merely a chance looker-on.

The idea bore more contemplation. He had behaved the perfect fool when he had visited with her parents and brothers, yet he was much more the Harry she had expected when it was only the two of them. What was so important that he must keep his true self hidden from her family? She felt that if she were to put the question to him when they were alone, he would as likely lie as not. She found she could not abide a liar but owned the possibility of secrets so important to be kept that the truth could not be shared. Depending on his reasons, she could find it in herself to forgive him.

Whatever the case may be, Mira knew one thing: she had felt sure he meant to kiss her as he stood at the window, and for the first time in her life, was rather afraid she had meant to kiss him back. The tumult that had started in her chest when she feared he might plunge to his death on the ground below had subsided a bit, though perhaps it only seemed so in comparison to the insistent fluttering in her belly. Pressing her hands to her stomach, she moved to the washstand to begin her morning ablutions, suddenly determined to look her best.

As she washed her face and combed her hair, she was set on accomplishing a number of other imperatives as well. First, she must discover what it was Harry was hiding, as well as answers to so many questions, such as why he has passed the night in the passage outside her room, and why he had again behaved as the tiresome Bertie. If the reasons for his sham performances were acceptable, and if he trusted her enough to tell her the truth, that was all she needed to feel confident that he was the man she wished to marry. When she was honest with herself, she admitted that he always had been. Next, she must discover the means to convince her parents of that fact. Last of all, though perhaps most imperative, was a much more pleasant task: to win Harry's heart.

With enticement in mind, Mira spent an inordinate amount of time over her *toilette* and refused to be rushed when her mother entered the room with a reminder that their journey would be resumed directly after breakfast. As it was clear her admonitions to be quick were falling on deaf ears, Lady Crenshaw took one of Mira's long, red curls in her hand and proceeded to pepper her daughter with questions as they pinned up her hair.

"Should you like your curls divided and off to each side or should we add a topknot at the crown?" Lady Crenshaw asked.

"A topknot, certainly!"

"And what about a ribbon? Blue to match your eyes or something to match your gown?"

Mira briefly considered the blue but finally decided on the green as it matched the color of the leaves on her bonnet to perfection.

Next were the difficult questions. "You are up rather early this morning. Did you not sleep well?"

"In fact, I did not. I should be surprised anyone did with all that commotion," Mira answered with a nonchalant air while analyzing her mother's face in the mirror for a reaction.

"I didn't hear a thing," Lady Crenshaw said, her expression above suspicion, "but I doubt I would have heard a gale outside my window what with the way your father snores!"

"No! Not Papa!" Mira bantered, her mind occupied with the questions her mother should be asking, such as: What were you doing under the table with Harry Haversham yesterday afternoon?

To Mira's great relief, her mother didn't ask but her next question was far from better. "You seem a bit anxious to look your best this morning. Is it on account of your cousin?"

Mira bit back the sharp denial that came to her tongue. When the time came, it wouldn't do at all for her mother to believe Mira had chosen Harry simply to escape marriage to George. Nor would it do for Lady Crenshaw to suppose that Mira was setting her cap for Harry, at least not at this point in her plans. "If I appear to be anxious, it is only in anticipation of arriving in London today. A girl has only one debutante Season, and I want everything to be flawless." She twisted about in her chair to face her mother who was obliged to hastily release a clutch of curls from her grasp. "Mama, you know how much I love you and Papa, do you not?"

"But, of course, my darling!" Lady Crenshaw dropped a kiss on her daughter's nose. "Goose! Why do you ask?"

Mira turned her attention to her reflection in the mirror and concentrated on holding still for the last few pins to anchor her coiffure. "It's only that I am grown up now and shall soon be married. It is not a decision I take lightly. If I am to leave you and Papa, it would only be if I thought I should be truly happy with someone else."

Lady Crenshaw caught her daughter's gaze in the mirror and held it with her own. "So, this *is* about George, is it not?"

"I suppose, to some extent," Mira admitted. "You know that I cannot abide him. Yet I do want to make you and Papa happy. Your happiness is my own."

"Your father and I would never wish you to sacrifice yourself for us," Lady Crenshaw insisted. "At the same time, it might surprise you how much better the older generation is at pairing men and women than we are ourselves," she said with a coquettish smile. "I never would have married your father if your great-grandmother hadn't taken steps."

Mira had often heard the story of how her parents greatly disliked one another prior to being thrown together by Great-Grandmama. Mira rather doubted the quoting of a few lines from Shakespeare's *The Tempest* at a house party forced upon the hosts by a pox quarantine could make her love George the way her mother and father loved one another. In the end, there was nothing about George she could find to love. He was knowledgeable but not in the least wise. He was somewhat handsome but not attractive, at least not in her eyes. He was rich, but Mira never cared much for the things money could buy, aside from beautiful clothes. Though it made her feel slightly ashamed of herself to think such a thing, Mira had to admit the problem was not in her ability to love but in his very nature.

"Mama," Mira asked as she took her mother's hand and rose to look her in the eyes. "Do you think you could have been as happy as you are now if you had married someone else?"

"Well," her mother said with a little laugh, "it wasn't as if I had any other offers. Not legitimate ones, anyway. I suppose if I had waited long enough, someone might have come along and taken pity on me."

"Oh, Mama, never say so! I am persuaded there were scores of gentleman who would have given money to marry you!"

With a wry smile, Lady Crenshaw shook her head and drew Mira down to sit on the bed beside her. "As to the question at hand, no, I do not think I would have been as happy as I am with your father and not only because I love him so much, as he does me. It has as much to do with the fact that loving him made me a better person, a person I could more easily live with as much as he. If I had married someone else—or not at all—I rather doubt I would have had enough reason to grow and change in the ways I have. So, really, it is about more than simply being with the person you love best. It is about becoming the person you can best live with as well."

"Oh, Mama," Mira said around the lump that had formed in her throat. "How could I even think of marrying and leaving you and Papa? It is so very difficult to believe that I could love someone enough to leave you or to change for him. Shouldn't I want my husband to love me for myself, just the way I am?"

"But of course!" Lady Crenshaw said, gathering her daughter in her arms and giving her a squeeze. "And any man would! Why, you are beautiful, accomplished, and intelligent. What more could a man want? The question is do *you* want more?"

With that, Lady Crenshaw stood and left her daughter to her thoughts, and troublesome thoughts they were. Was she only so against marriage to George because she would have to change in order to be happy with him? Could Mama be right in that she knew better who was best for her daughter? Or did she yearn for Harry because she knew, deep down inside, he would inspire her to become a better person if only he could somehow love her?

There was one way to learn the truth. Surely this willingness to grow and change for the one you loved worked both ways. She would simply go to Harry's room, knock on his door, and ask him why he was found asleep in the passage outside her bedchamber. If he answered her question with the honest truth, she would take it as a sign that he cared for her enough to forever change from the deplorable Bertie to the Harry she knew lurked inside.

She slipped into her shoes, hastened down the passageway to the room he had indicated belonged to him, and knocked boldly on the door. She could hardly swallow her disappointment when the man who answered the door wasn't Harry at all, but the vacuous and intolerable Bertie, a fatuous smile fixed to his face and a quantity of lace at his chin and wrists. He stood, frozen with shock or some other nameless emotion, one hand on his hip and a foot turned out as if he were about to produce a pirouette. It was a stance she had always felt looked odd enough in dancing slippers but was utterly laughable in riding boots. However, she refused to give up so readily.

Taking a deep breath, she rallied enough to ask what she had come to learn. "Lord Haversham, I find I cannot rest until I learn the answer to this question. Why did you sleep outside my door last night?" There, it was out and he must answer, one way or another. She prayed she would be able to hear his response above the pounding of her heart.

"Why, Miss Crenshaw, my dear girl! Don't you know, it's what all the Parisian fellows do these days," he said with a flip of his wrist. "They find the loveliest girl in the inn and they sleep outside her door. It's terribly gallant, don't you think?"

It was a pretty answer, but Mira knew it to be a lie. Her disappointment now too great to hide, she felt her face fall. In fact, she was persuaded every muscle in her body had turned to jelly. Before she could put a hand against the wall to steady herself, he was there to balance her in his arms, and she found herself suddenly in his room with the door shut behind them.

"Perceptive girl, I should have known I could never throw dust in your eyes long enough to deceive you about anything at all whatsoever," he said, gazing earnestly into her face. "In point of fact, I did know it, which is why I was determined to stay as far away from you as possible," he admitted as he assisted her into the chair alongside his bed, which, she noticed, had not been slept in.

"But, Harry, why?" she asked, her heart beginning to again hammer in her chest. She sensed rather than saw the way the muscles in his shoulders tensed as he turned away from her.

"Why must I lie to you? Pretend to be someone I am not?"

She nodded, and he began to pace the bit of rug between the bed and the fireplace while she waited.

Finally, he threw his hands in the air and said, "I can't. I simply am not at liberty to explain why I must keep secrets from you. Perhaps one day I shall." Kneeling at her feet, he took her hands in his. "You have always stood my friend and I must beg you to continue to do so," he urged, his eyes glittering with unshed tears.

Before she could form a reply, he rose to his feet and once again turned from her to stand with his hands braced against the mantel. "What might I do to convince you of my sincerity?"

Mira had never in all her life felt such an intense range of emotions in so short a space of time. One minute her heart was pounding, the next it hung like lead in her chest. Every time her hopes had been lifted, they had been as equally dashed, and now he twisted her into pieces with a sorrow that seemed so genuine. However, if he could truthfully answer her original question with as much authentic feeling as he even now exhibited, she would give him the benefit of the doubt and wait with patience for the day when he could tell her all.

"It is true, we have always been friends. and it is my dearest wish we might remain so, though, as you must have guessed, I have no use for your Bertie."

"As I would have had no use for you should you have taken a shine to him," Harry said with a rueful laugh.

She rose to her feet and reached out to lay her hand on his arm but snatched it back. In spite of all the familiar interactions they enjoyed when they were young, to touch him now, if even in the same careless way, felt like a promise rather than a mere gesture. She pressed her hands together against her once again fluttering stomach and imposed her conditions. "I understand you feel you mustn't tell me what is happening or why. Though I do not like it, I can see that you are sincerely distressed. It is not my wish to deepen that distress, yet I find I need some indication of your veracity. You need not tell me all; I merely wish to know the answer to a single question and should you tell me true, I will wait for the answers to the others for as long as you need keep them from me."

Slowly he turned to face her, his mouth a grim line even as hope lightened the shadows in his eyes. "Ask and I shall answer, but only if I am free to do so, in which case it will be God's truth, I so swear it."

Now that the moment was at hand, Mira felt oddly reluctant. She knew her questions would reveal her feelings but she dared not trust him with something so precious as of yet. Perhaps it would be safer if her questions sounded chosen at random. "I suppose it would be most useful to ask why you have requested to be called Bertie and why you sometimes behave like a buffoon, however, based on the shadow that has just crossed your face, I daresay you would not answer me that one."

"In that you would be most correct," he said with a tiny smile of relief.

"There is always the matter of the pistol I saw half hidden in the folds of your clothing this morning, but that seems a most personal matter and one which you would likely find not for my delicate ears."

Harry gave her an arch look. "What is amiss about a man arming himself?"

"Pity. I have learned that it isn't always preferable to be right."

"If that is your question, I have answered it truthfully. That is, as truthfully as I can," he said, spreading his hands in entreaty.

"I might ask why you kissed me yesterday." It was an audacious question, and her heart pounded a bit harder than to what she was accustomed.

"For the same reason I kissed you all those years ago. I beg your pardon for implying I had forgotten it; I have not."

"That is not an answer," she fired back.

"Isn't it?" he asked softly, chaining her gaze with his own. "It is clear as day to me."

For a moment, she felt so disordered in her brain that she failed to recollect her specific query and would have thrown herself into his arms without another word. One corner of reason remained, however, and it reminded her that lies fell easily from his lips. She must ask her question, and he must answer true before she turned her heart over to him. "Why, then, did you sleep outside my door last night?" she asked, bowing her head to prevent his looking into her face to read what was written there.

He laughed, a pleasant sound full of ease. "Are you sure that is the one you want to know? It is quite simple, really. You were in danger, and I meant to protect you. That is all."

"I? In danger?" Mira asked, incredulous.

"But of course. Did I not just say so?"

"You can't mean from my cousin? Surely not! He is weak and tedious but along with that comes cowardice. He would never force himself upon me."

"No?" he asked and drew a deep breath. "I am most relieved. But, in truth, that is not the danger of which I spoke."

It was clear that he was preparing to reveal a secret, and the very idea sent a trill of delight along her spine.

"I am in service to the Qu . . ." he said, hesitating, "rather, I am involved in something . . . something thoroughly honorable that I wish I could share with you, but I cannot. I ought not but I will tell you that I was the target of yesterday's shooting. Either that or Higgins was. Or rather, both of us. At any rate, there are those who want me dead," he said shortly. "I didn't care so much for myself," he added, his voice shaking a trifle, "but knowing that I had put you and your most esteemed parents in danger was too much to bear."

Mira, too stunned to speak, sat with her mouth open in a most unladylike fashion.

"I see that you don't believe me, but Mira, it is true. I wish it weren't so, but it is and it's all I can say. Meanwhile, my being here, still, with you in this inn, puts you in danger, but . . . . I simply couldn't bring myself to leave you." He paused and closed his eyes, then opened them again with a sigh. "That is why I slept outside your door last night, to protect you even as I was increasing your danger by so doing. Will you forgive me for my weakness?"

Very quietly, Mira stood and held out her hand to him. Taking it in his, he kissed it with a fervency that felt as real as anything as Mira had ever known. Gently, she drew it away and without a word, opened the door and shut it behind her, her heart hammering in her chest. She thought he had been about to say that he was in service to the Queen. Could he have meant the Queen of *England*? Surely not! There was nothing left to do now but leave Harry alone with his deceit for she had never heard such a pack of lies in all her life.

chapter six

Harry had never been so indiscreet in all his life. What was it about Mira that caused him to come so undone? He had let slip too much, more than he should have, more, even, than was safe, yet far less than he wished. If she guessed the truth as to his mission in the Queen's secret service . . . should she spread it about . . . the consequences did not bear thinking on.

Once the door had closed behind her and she had descended the stairs to take breakfast, he felt it safe to quit the room, accompanied by a better hidden pistol, to check the passageway for signs of anything untoward. He then took the servants' stairs to the kitchen and on out the back door to do a circuit of the grounds before he returned to his room and down the proper set of stairs to the dining room where he found the entire Crenshaw family seated just as they had been the afternoon prior.

"I bid you a ravishing good morning!" he chirped in his best Bertie intonations. "It would seem there is something especially welcoming about this table as it's the selfsame one at which you were seated yesterday." He favored Mira with a hint of a smile in memory of how he had kissed her under said selfsame table, but she looked pointedly away, staring at her cup of hot chocolate as if it had grown horns.

"You are not wrong," George stated with his usual arrogance.

"Come, have some coffee," Lady Crenshaw insisted.

"Delighted," Harry said. "I find there was a dreadful racket all the night long. I'm simply exhausted! It shall require nothing less than an entire pot to put me to rights." As Lady Crenshaw poured out a steaming cup, Harry stole another glance at Mira to see if she appreciated this reference to her interrupted night's sleep, but she had turned pointedly away from him and was now staring at her cousin as if the sudden growth of a set of horns had spread to him from the crockery.

"George," she said, "it is rumored that you have bought another race horse."

"Yes, a Thoroughbred of the finest quality," he replied with a nod. "I had intended to race him at the next assize-week, but I find I am needed in London."

"But of course you intend to appear for at least a portion of this year's Season, Your Grace," Lady Crenshaw admonished, "as it is Mira's come-out." She gave her husband a bit of a nudge to the elbow whereupon he echoed his wife's sentiments.

"It wouldn't be a London Season without the Duke of Marcross, would it?" he replied with all the charm for which Sir Anthony was noted. Though he was nobody's sycophant, Harry knew Mira's father to have the tidiest manners of his class.

"Naturally, it is for Mira's come-out that I dashed about so in order to be ready in time, but I do regret leaving behind Witch's Brew," George said without the slightest thought for Mira's feelings. This time, when Harry stole a glance at her, she met his gaze in a moment of affable accord before looking away again with a jerk.

"Such a love story!" Harry said with a sip of his coffee. "I wager Witch's Brew misses you more than anyone, those present not to be excluded. In point of fact, I should go so far as to suggest that Miss Crenshaw feels the pain of that cruel separation more than most."

Mira, her cup to her lips, attempted to hide her sudden mirth, but Harry knew she needn't have spared the feelings of the Duke who continued to speak of her as if she were anywhere but seated across the table from him.

"Miss Crenshaw, as always, has my best interests at heart," he said. "It is for this reason, as well as my father's wish, that I find her an acceptable choice as my bride." He would have said more save for the clatter of porcelain cups being hurriedly joined to their saucers all around the table.

Harry was a bit taken aback by the reaction of the Crenshaws as he had feared Mira's betrothal to her cousin to be a *fait accompli.* Hope rose a bit in his heart as he assessed the faces around him. Sir Anthony looked mildly surprised, as if he hadn't expected quite so precipitate an announcement. That, at least, was something in Harry's favor. Lady Crenshaw bore a look of long-suffering as if she wasn't entirely sure she approved of a match between her daughter and the Duke, a nearly unquestionable vote against it. Mira, however, looked as if she simply hadn't heard what George had said as she once again took up her cup and swallowed the dregs of her hot chocolate.

"I believe that's the last of my breakfast," she said with a cheery smile. "Shall we be on our way?"

"Oh, but Haaaa . . . Bertie hasn't had a bite to eat," Lady Crenshaw said.

"Really?" Mira asked. "What a pity as I am persuaded he is possessed of a strong desire to be seated inside the carriage this morning, and it seems as if George shall most likely get there first."

Harry was jerked from his feigned somnolence by this pronouncement. Why, it was almost as if Mira wished to be seated next to George all the day long. And here Harry thought that they had an understanding after his making a clean breast of things such a short time ago. Nearly a clean breast, rather. He looked a question at Mira and was answered by a look of challenge in return.

Could she be playing at seeming disinterested in him? If so, it was not Mira's usual style. Unlike most young ladies of Harry's acquaintance, she was the sort of girl who said what she meant and meant what she said. It was one of the qualities he loved best in her. He tossed his napkin to the table and rose to his feet whilst he attempted to remember just what it was she did say after he had confessed to her so much more than he should have.

He was so engaged with his thoughts, he barely noticed George had already risen to his feet and taken Mira by the arm. They were fully out in the yard before Harry realized he lagged behind the entire group, that he had, with Mira's acceptance and perhaps even approval, lost out on being seated beside her for the duration and that he, as of yet, had not bespoken his mount. By the time the horse was saddled and Harry mounted, the Crenshaw carriage was all but lost behind a cloud of dust.

Harry considered breaking his whip on his horse's back in order to catch them up but was too occupied with the question of what exactly had gone wrong to put any further plan into action. He had told her all he could, more, even, than he should have and had believed her to understand. Even if she did not hold him in the highest regard, she would surely prefer him by her side in the carriage than her cousin any day of the week, of this Harry was quite certain.

He owned once again that it wasn't like Mira to play games, but it seemed she was doing exactly that. Faced with the prospect of a long day in the saddle alongside the carriage with nothing but hope to sustain him held little allure. Instead, he could be in London hours ahead of them as he drew danger away from those he esteemed as well as his own family—better, even. As such, Harry decided to sheer off and complete his journey the way he had started it: entirely alone.

Upon his arrival in the city, Harry rode directly to Claridge's, opting to delay paying a call to Haversham House to face his mother's displeasure at his decision to lodge elsewhere to some point in the future, the further away the better. Once ensconced in his room as private citizen Samuel Linford, he was free to eat a hearty meal by the fire, without danger of being tripped, shot at, or slapped under the table. That being said, he was more than happy to admit he had yet to pass the time under a table so pleasantly, even when he took into account his rainy day fort-building with the Holland covers as a boy.

As the promised coded knock at the door did not immediately occur, Harry was free to reflect on the conundrum of his situation; he was in love with a girl who placed much stock in truth, whilst he earned his daily bread by concealing the very fact that he was employed and by whom. It was enough to undo the sternest of men. By the second day of confinement, apprehensive and unable to do anything about his ailing heart or his assignment, Harry was up for just about anything. When a scratch at the door came at nearly twelve of the clock on a moonless night, he was dressed, armed to the hilt and ready for anything as long as it meant moving forward.

Donning his greatcoat against the damp of a May night, he descended the hotel stairs and let himself out the front door with a borrowed key. The fact that he hadn't permission nor the owner knowledge of his having lent it had naught to do with anything. The Queen must be protected at any cost, and the temporary loss of a key was nothing. The possible sacrifice of a life spent with Mira was not so easily dismissed, but dismiss it for the moment, he must.

He worked his way around to the mews as quickly as he dared and saddled his horse with such stealth even the stable hand hadn't a notion he had been saved the trouble. He then walked the horse down the lane through the mud of the verge so as to muffle the noise of his departure and waited to mount until he was well down the road. Only then did he think to wonder how many miles he would need go that night and when he might again see his bed.

He was tempted to wonder as well when he might see Mira again, but he forced the thought aside. He had no idea what would come of this night, where his next assignment would take him, and when. He might have only enough time in London to settle his bill before he was required to head off to parts unknown. Aware that he had given the Crenshaws the impression that he was in London for the Season, he fervently hoped it were true, but what if duty called elsewhere? How could he leave her now?

Without warning, the skies opened, and the rain poured down as if in accompaniment to his woe. He urged his horse to run faster, ducked his head deeper into his collar, and raced through the night towards the Richmond bridge.

By the time he sighted the towering Pagoda, his hat and coat were as wet as if he had plunged into the river itself, but at least the rain had stopped. He slowed his horse to a trot, entered the grounds of the gardens and headed for the Pagoda, relieved that the height of the tower made it visible in spite of the black night. He found a stand of trees in which to hide his mount, hobbled it, and reached into his pocket for a handful of raisins. While the horse enjoyed its treat, Harry studied the area for anything untoward but he could see very little below the heavily shadowed tree line. Pulling out his pistol, he cocked it, and moved into the inky blackness with an arm outstretched.

It seemed a small eternity before he came in contact with the rough brick of the Pagoda, but he had made it and with only one minor stumble when his boot hit the foundation. With his pistol in his right hand and the fingers of his left brushing against the outer wall, he went round the circular building and listened for any signs of life; he was rewarded with the echo of boots striking the inner staircase, step by step. Though he daren't assume the person inside the Pagoda was his secret service contact, he moved forward without hesitation when he heard a faint nicker of a horse just as his hand brushed against what he hoped to be the entrance.

If Harry remembered his history aright, the Pagoda was over one hundred and fifty feet tall, and more than two hundred and fifty steps would have to be taken before he reached the last of ten floors, making this the most tedious part of his night. The steps were steep and his need for stealth great, so he took his time, especially since the interior was black as pitch. Shafts of paler dark spilled through the windows of each floor, but as the staircase was in the center of the building, it did little to illuminate his path.

He counted each floor as he reached it, and just when he thought his thigh muscles would fail before he gained the final floor, he heard something that didn't sound quite right. He stopped dead in his tracks, brought his pistol up, and listened. The sound was muffled, but gradually he realized he heard a conversation, one between two men. He was to meet but one. Instantly, he dropped to a crouch and crawled a few steps higher so as to better hear what was being said.

"It wouldn't matter if you were the Queen herself," came a voice Harry had never before heard. "You shan't have the paper until you give me the password."

What was this? Surely these weren't Harry's orders under discussion!

"You are being overcautious, sir. I am precisely who I say I am and I must insist on having that letter!"

With this utterance Harry broke out into a sweat so sudden, his pistol nearly slipped from his hand. He strained his eyes in the darkness in hopes of locating exactly where the two men stood so as to better ascertain a suitable place to hide, as hiding was his best option; one could hardly shoot dead the Duke of Marcross, even if Harry could see him well enough to hit him.

"What are you waiting for, man!" George continued. "Surely you cannot doubt a duke. I must have that paper this instant!" he hissed just loudly enough to cover Harry's ascent of the final steps to the top floor landing, whereupon there came a low thud followed by a louder one as, Harry assumed, his secret service contact fell to the floor.

Harry had just enough time to slip to one side of the top stair and take cover in the inky shadows against the far wall before George rushed the staircase and fled with a clatter that Harry could only wonder at; surely, were George a traitor, he should be at as many pains to shield his identity as was Harry. How the Duke had managed to follow Harry and get ahead of him on the stairs of the Pagoda was a mystery as was why George should wish to.

Harry brooded on these questions as he made his way to the man lying on the floor and groaning in pain. Harry removed his riding gloves and fingered the man's head until he felt a quantity of warm, sticky blood. Relief washed over him as further investigation revealed that the injury was not serious.

"The orders . . ." the man murmured as his head turned from side to side between Harry's hands.

"Where are they?" Harry demanded and abandoned the man for a proper search of the floor around him. "They're not here," he barked, moving his search from the floor to the man's hands and pockets.

"I can't . . . I can't give 'em to you without the password," the man said with a groan.

"Now that is something I do have," Harry countered. "But first you must put the question to me."

"Sure, and you're right," the man muttered, followed by the sounds of his getting to his feet and moving towards the far wall of the tower. Harry could hear him fumbling with what must have been a lantern and a flint to light the candle inside. Within a moment, a flame flared into life, and Harry was face to face with his contact. "The question," he said, "is this: *Quae est Regina nostra?*"

Harry returned the answer in Latin as well. "*Ipsa est, nulli nisi Victoria.*"

"Just so," said the man. "But I can't give you your orders as I don't have them."

"Don't have them?" Harry all but shouted. "Don't tell me that coward actually managed to make off with them!"

"He did at that," the man replied with a shake of his head. "But I still needed to be sure you were legitimate as I have this for you as well." He handed Harry a thick packet of vellum with the red seal of Lord Melbourne. "To whom it is to be delivered and when is included in your orders."

Harry drew a deep sigh and got to his feet. "Well, then, I am off to fetch them back. Report this incident to your contact and assure him I will get this sorted out." Harry paused to take a last look at the man's wound, and satisfied it was not in the least fatal, drew his gloves over his bloodied fingers. "I suppose it would be too much to ask if you were verbally made privy to my orders," Harry said as he returned his abandoned weapon to his belt.

"Nay," the man replied with a shake of his grizzled head. "They were in Latin."

"Latin!" Harry exclaimed in disbelief.

"Wot? You read Latin, doncha?"

"Yes, of course." All wellborn, titled schoolboys possessed of a goodly inheritance and a privileged family did. As such it did a fine job of narrowing down the possibilities as to his possible identity. He could hardly absorb the thought that George was a traitor to his country and preferred to assume his appearance at the tower was more of a misguided attempt to put a spoke in the wheels of Harry's endeavors. Perhaps George was even clever enough to view Harry as competition for Mira's favor, in spite of 'Bertie.'"

Nevertheless, George was the last person Harry trusted with sensitive information. And if George had somehow known enough to follow Harry to Richmond . . . It was a thought that filled him with dread.

"I hadn't tho't of that," the man said. "The password, it's in Latin, too."

"Yes, but that's hardly here nor there, is it? That's just between us," Harry said as he paced the bit of floor visible under the glow of the lantern.

"So were the orders, until that duke scarpered our meet."

"Yes, about that," Harry said, rubbing the back of his head. "We can feel confident that an eminent peer of the realm would not be fool enough to reveal himself as such." The fact that the Duke of Marcross did just that was all of a piece. "Clearly, it's just a cover, one that a true duke would not appreciate, were he to know."

"Come to think of it," Harry's companion mused, "he was a right unpleasant fellow, not what you would think of as a duke a'tall."

"Ha!" Harry said with a bark of laughter. "Then you have had little dealings with dukes," he revealed, then chided himself for his frame of mind. Protecting the identity of the Duke was of paramount importance, at least until Harry could ascertain his innocence of anything but severe petulance. However, if he found George to be a traitor to his country, Harry would draw and quarter him with his own two hands. But could Mira forgive him if he did so? The thought led to a melancholy of such force, it took him by surprise.

"Unpleasant or no," Harry said carefully, "you would look a fool if you were to report that a peer of the realm was the villain in this piece." He took up the lantern and handed it to his companion. "I believe this is yours," he said. "You had better be off and get that head cleaned up."

The man did so, and Harry stood at the top of the stairs, watching until the light of the lantern as it swung to and fro, dimmed a bit, then a bit more, then finally disappeared through the main floor door and out of sight. It was not a journey of a few moments and it gave Harry time to reflect on what his next steps should be. Would it be best to confront the Duke directly or wait until Harry had more information to go on? Though it was hard to believe George cared much for anything but himself, it was entirely possible he was in the power of those with more information and far less scruples, misguided but earnest men who felt the young Queen Victoria too weak a monarch for the throne of England. The rumor of an impending betrothal to Prince Albert of Saxe-Coburg-Gotha was an even less welcome prospect to those who were weary of the Teutonic reign. As such, a chilling decision had been arrived at, one which caused Harry's blood to boil: the young Queen should be murdered before her popularity had grown enough to translate into martyrdom at her death.

The thought lent wings to Harry's feet, and he dashed down the stairs and was on his horse, out of the shadow of the Pagoda, and over the bridge before he realized he hadn't the faintest idea where he should go next. A glance up into the gray and lavender-streaked sky indicated that dawn would be fully upon him in a matter of hours. Suddenly, it seemed imperative to plan his next steps with a steaming cup of tea at hand and his feet resting on the fender of a cheerful fire. It was far too long before he could make his thoughts a reality, but once he had changed into his dressing gown and bespoken a pot of tea, he thought he just might live.

As his feet thawed, a plan began to form in his mind. It was risky, fool-hardy, and quite possibly dreadfully insane but anything that involved the person he must make his confidant was bound to be a few shades beyond the pale. Still, it was the best he could do without involving the Crenshaws, whose safety must come before all others—even his mother's.

chapter seven

The evening of her family's departure from the Cygnet and Lute, Mira sat in her room at Wembley House in London wondering if perhaps she hadn't been too hard on Harry earlier that morning. Bertie or no, Harry would have proved a more amicable traveling companion than George. Besides, which, she hadn't meant to treat Harry so inconsiderately and hadn't realized she had done so until her mother took her to task once they were arrived and out of earshot of the men.

"For, Mira, you must know how your words at breakfast must have hurt him," she had said. "I don't believe I have ever seen such a purely *naked* look on Harry's face in all his life."

Mira could think of little to say in response except to point out that they hadn't seen him in ever so long, and that perhaps this particular expression was as commonplace as his ridiculous waistcoats, and that surely her mother had meant to use the word 'transparent' instead of 'naked' which clearly had unwelcome connotations. Rather than be filled with the sense of superiority she always felt when supplying a more exceptional word, she felt hollow inside and hadn't the faintest idea why. Now she was left alone in her room at Wembley House, her thoughts filled with doubt, wiping away tears for which she could not account.

Dinner brought new opportunities, however. The contemplation of her new ball gown—a tulle robe over a white satin slip—led her to square her shoulders and dry her tears. She wished to look her best in the case her mother had thought to invite Harry to dinner. Perhaps if he could abandon 'Bertie,' she might find it in her heart to forgive him for his lies. She might even become accustomed to his new manner of dress if only his features were arranged just as Harry had always used to wear them.

As she rose from her dressing table, she took up her fan and handbag, her spirits rising along with the rustling of her skirts as she closed the door behind her. When she spied her mother coming down the hall, all the unpleasantness of earlier in the afternoon was forgotten.

"Oh, Mama! How young and beautiful you look!" Mira exclaimed.

"Nowhere near as do you," Lady Crenshaw said with a warm smile.

"I am persuaded the gentlemen at the ball will assume us sisters, each and every one," Mira insisted and took her mother's hand as they proceeded down the stairs to dinner. "Which calls something to mind. Have you invited Harry to dinner?"

"I'm so sorry, dearest, I had meant to but I hadn't the chance. I had assumed he would be riding into London with us and I would have many opportunities to speak to him about it. It is a pity that I did not."

"I . . . I had thought so as well." Mira hoped her face did not betray her sudden misery. She knew he had gone ahead on account of her behavior and wished she knew if he were angry as well as hurt. Now she would not be able to beg his pardon until the ball; it seemed an eternity to wait.

"Don't look so downcast, Mira. I have invited George to dinner. He will be escorting us to the ball as your father has business to attend to this evening."

There was no reply to this piece of news Mira could speak aloud as they had reached the bottom of the stairs in full view of her family, and she wished not to invite ridicule from her brothers. However, her dismay was tangible. An entire day seated by George in the carriage, his well-oiled hair accosting her view whenever she looked up and his bony fingers spread across his knees whenever she looked down, was enough punishment for her unkindness to Harry at breakfast. Must she spend the evening with him as well? Could she possibly endure marriage to him?

There came a rap at the door, and Mira's heart took up a startling tattoo in her breast. Perhaps Harry had come after all. Surely he would assume he was always welcome just as he used to. She let go of her mother's hand and waited in the hall until their guest entered, every fiber of her being alive with anticipation. It was with a decided decline of her spirits that she saw it was only George after all.

"Miss Crenshaw," he said with a nod of his head, as if she were a mere acquaintance rather than the woman he had chosen to make his wife.

"George, thank you for coming," Mira said with a smile even as her heart sank. "Mama says you are to be our escort to the ball this evening as Papa cannot attend."

"Horses couldn't drag me from your side," George replied.

"None but Witch's Brew," Mira retorted with a flash of annoyance. Had he not said as much at breakfast that very day?

George frowned and took her by the elbow to force her to his side. "A temper such as that is not becoming, Mira. I hope never to see such a lapse again," he hissed in her ear as he led her into the dining room and seated her at her father's left. George took his seat on her father's right, as was his due, a circumstance that left Mira nowhere to look except straight at his needled nose during the course of the meal. Instead, she fumed into her plate and consoled herself with thoughts of her father's rage when he learned of George's behavior. However, there would not be the time to tell him of it until tomorrow. She prayed it would be soon enough to put paid to George's suit for her hand in marriage, or delay it at the very least.

Adrian and Stephen took up seats on either side of the table, and Mama her usual seat at the end. "George," she said, "I am given to understand that you have made a substantial contribution to one of the Queen's charities. How exemplary of you!"

"Those in my position must do what one can," he replied. He picked up his spoon and dipped it into his soup bowl. "While we are on that note, I trust that before too long, dear Cousin, you will become accustomed to giving me my due, even in such familial surroundings."

Mira felt as if her eyes flew of their own accord to note her mother's reaction. Her face looked as if it had crumpled, and her ears were as rosy as her cheeks. "I beg pardon, Your Grace," she said. "It's only that I have known you since you were an infant. I hadn't thought how you are addressed would be of any consequence, here, amongst ourselves. However, I shall do as you wish, of course."

A moment of pregnant silence ensued, followed by the crash of Adrian's fist to the table. "That is coming it a bit strong, George!" he exclaimed. "Are Stephen and I to tug at our forelocks as well?"

"But of course not," George asserted. "Though of a decidedly lower social circle, you are Crenshaws, as is my cousin Anthony. That applies to you as well, Mira," he said with a nod of his head in her direction.

"Pray forgive me should I not thank you for the honor of calling you by your given name," Mira snapped. "Papa, I wonder that you should have naught to say," she prodded with a look for her father who appeared to be every bit as angry as Mira felt.

"George is young and in want of guidance in this matter," he said in a voice so even as to be positively ominous. "Let it not be forgotten, Your Grace, that my wife is your cousin on the Wembley side, and it is through her hospitality that you are seated at this table. Ginny, my love, I find that I must hurry if I am to keep my appointment," he said as he rose and went to her side. "I regret that it is not I who shall be escorting the loveliest lady at the ball," he added in low tones, whereupon he kissed her hand, bowed, and quit the room without a look or word for the rest of his family.

"Well then, shall we eat?" Lady Crenshaw chirped with a wave of her fork and a sparkle in her eye. Her sons turned to their plates with alacrity and betrayed no sign that they had observed the tight compression of George's already too-thin lips. However, Mira did notice, along with the way the blood had drained from his face, his complexion now a hue somewhere between winding sheet-gray and curdled milk-white.

It seemed that lightening the mood was to be left to her. "Will the ball be very crowded, Mama?"

"I suppose it shall," her mother replied. "It is the first of the season and sure to be a grand affair. Never fear, my darling, you will take very well, I am persuaded of that, and shall have many opportunities to dance," she added, her face beaming.

"At least I might be assured of three dances, may I not?" Mira asked with a look for each of the young men seated at table. She reached into her drawstring bag and drew forth a dance card. "Isn't it the cunningest little thing? It was included in the invitation. Do you not see, George?" she asked in a vain attempt to wheedle him into a semblance of good humor. "I shall give you first choice of the dances. I know that there are some of which you are not fond." She placed the little book on the table and waited as he took a pencil from his breast pocket and wrote his name, not once, as she expected, but thrice.

"Why, George, that is most generous of you," Mira said in her brightest voice. "However, by three, I had meant one for each of you."

"It is customary for a gentleman to have the opening and closing waltz with his lady, as well as the March," George replied in his usual top-lofty tones.

Mira bit her lip. Would there be a waltz left for Harry? She did so wish to speak with him and, to be sure, the waltz was the most promising opportunity for audible conversation.

"Well!" Stephen exclaimed. "She is as much my lady as yours, George, as no announcement of your betrothal has been made. It might seem a bit odd, in fact, should you claim three whole dances of an evening." He withdrew his own pencil and scribbled in the little book, whereupon he passed it to Adrian, who scribbled his own name in turn and returned it to Mira with a wink.

Mira was gratified to see that he had crossed out George's name and claimed the March for himself. Stephen had done the same with the last waltz. She had barely time to note this, however, before George pulled the card from her fingers.

"Am I to have only one dance with you then?" he demanded.

"There are many dances yet to fill," she replied, suppressing an urge to snatch the card and allow him only the first waltz. "Why, there is the Quadrille and the Cotillion and a contradanse."

George gazed at her with a narrow-eyed look. "I know what it is you are about. You are hoping to save the waltzes for Lord Haversham, are you not?"

"It would be odd should she not reserve a dance for him," Lady Crenshaw interrupted. "He is one of her oldest friends. Besides which, this is Mira's first official ball, and I won't see the three of you cluttering up her dance card. There will be any number of young men vying for the chance to dance with her, and I, for one, will enjoy watching events unfold."

"I must confess, I have yet to speak to Mira's father," George said with another nod at his intended. "However, once the betrothal is announced, I expect to claim my privileges."

"Just so long as by privileges you mean two waltzes and the March, there will be no need for pistols at dawn," Stephen said with a snort.

"If you are implying that Mira and I should anticipate our vows," George said in clipped tones, "I should think that to be none of your affair."

"What it is Stephen meant to imply," Adrian said as he leaned across the table to better facilitate staring down his cousin, "is just this: if you so much as touch Mira without her consent, betrothed or no, you will have to answer to us."

"Pray abandon this topic of conversation before you offend the ladies," George demanded.

"It is your attitude that most offends me, George," Lady Crenshaw said with a challenging lift of her eyebrow.

Mira thought her mother never looked more regal, her brothers never so handsome, and George never so like he had swallowed a toad. For the remainder of the meal, not a soul opened his or her mouth for any purpose but that of the forking of food. At one point, Mira considered screaming so as to break up the heavy silence but owned that her father would be horrified should she do so in his presence and deemed his absence no excuse for such a breach of conduct.

Eventually, it was time to board the carriage for the journey to the ancestral pile of the lord and lady who would host the ball. As expected, George took Mira's arm to lead her through to the front hall. Adrian took the other only long enough to whisper in her ear.

"Should Harry be at the ball, I shall give him my waltz," he said, before dropping behind to take his mother's arm. Mira felt her heart swell with gratitude, whereupon, Stephen took his place and whispered, "Why you should wish to dance with such a jackanapes, I will never know."

"To which jackanapes do you refer?" she hissed back, to which Stephen merely gave her a wry grin and dropped behind to take his mother's free arm until they had made their way outdoors and began to board the carriage. Mira felt she had sat beside George in one conveyance or another long enough to last a lifetime, but, naturally, he had other ideas and forced her mother and brothers to sit together on the seat that faced backwards.

"George, is it not ill-done of us to take the forward facing seat when my mother must sit on the other?" Mira asked in hopes that he would be gallant and offer to switch with his hostess.

"Doubtless Lady Crenshaw appreciates your loyalty," George retorted, "but you really must accustom yourself to your new status. As my Duchess, you shall take precedence over your mother, as well as your brothers and well-esteemed papa. I am persuaded that even your mama would not dare to voice a differing opinion on this subject."

Mira sensed rather than saw three sets of jaws tighten at his words and knew the response to this piece of folly was best left to her. "I do not believe status to be an adequate substitute for manners," Mira said with a mildness she did not feel. "It seems to me that as a suitor to my hand, you would have the decency to treat my mother with the respect due any lady in her circumstances."

"I take your point with regards to your mother. As to your use of the word 'suitor,' let it be understood that matters have progressed beyond the need for such descriptions. To say so would be to imply there are others competing for your hand in marriage and that is not the case. That is to say, should there be any, your father will most assuredly put paid to their pretensions as you and I have been promised to one another since you were a child."

Mira heard the release of a frustrated sigh from one of her brothers, she knew not which, and took heart. "I understand you believe that to be the case, but I am correct in assuming no official contract has been made. Tomorrow, once I have made my bows to the Queen, I shall be officially out and as likely as any other of the girls making their debut this Season to be favored."

"It is quite true, my darling," her mother piped in before George, who had turned red with rage, had a chance to speak. "You are sure to meet with little competition. Not only shall you outshine the other debutantes his year, you are bound to be outnumbered by the young men, the occupants of this carriage a case in point. The years prior to your birth were replete with baby boys, or so it seemed. I warrant there will be half a dozen young men laying claim to the hand of each young lady."

"Mother," Adrian implored, "you make it sound as if Mira were a broodmare rather than a young lady *en route* to her first ball. Furthermore, the thought of just such a conversation going on in the carriages of young ladies all over London, also *en route* to this ball, causes me to quake in my boots. Should I consider a compliment a declaration? Should I only request a dance from those young ladies I wish to regard me as a suitor? Am I even now to weep and gnash my teeth with the knowledge that young ladies of marriageable age are few and far between and I should therefore plan my strategy accordingly?"

At this final utterance, Stephen could no longer contain his mirth. "As if a one of them would let you near! Why should they look to you when your vastly more eligible older brother stands at the ready to sweep them off their feet?"

"Oh dear," their mother mused. "I hadn't considered either of you old enough to become serious about finding a wife as of yet. It seems like only yesterday the both of you were in leading strings. A young lady wants an older man, one slightly more mature and definitely established, for a husband. What is more, should she be so foolish as to let her heart wholly rule her head, she doubtless has a father to set her straight."

"Is that how you ended up with Papa?" her eldest twitted her. "With no father to see you wed to one of his cronies, you were allowed to marry for love, is that not so?"

"That is neither here nor there," their mother insisted. "Besides, my Grandaunt Regina was far more formidable than *anyone's* father. It was her dearest wish to see your papa and I married. We were fortunate in that we suited one another and that your father had the means to support me in spite of his youth."

"Suited? Is that what you call it?" Adrian hooted. "If that's the case, things seem to have deteriorated into all-out infatuation since."

"Mama and Papa were madly in love!" Mira exclaimed.

"Not at the outset," her mother replied, "but certainly by the time he offered marriage, there was little doubt as to how either of us felt. That being said, he had more than a few pennies to rub together at the time. Love is a powerful motivator, but one can hardly live on it."

George's high coloring had receded, but Mira could sense his agitation despite the distance forced between them by the hoops of her skirt. She hadn't any idea what it was about their topic of conversation that offended him but she knew that it hardly mattered. They were bound to disagree on almost everything.

Memories of Harry, recent ones, began to fill her mind, in particular the expression on his face just that morning when she had so callously denied him a seat by her side in the carriage. A shaft of longing pierced her heart with such suddenness, it was all she could do not to cry out. She took up her fan and began to wield it with a vengeance. Perhaps if the draft became stiff enough, it would blow away her desire to see Harry, at least for the time being.

Upon their arrival at the party, they were ushered into the ballroom of the enormous house, quite out of the usual for London where most families of quality made do with a townhouse squeezed between two others and across the square from a row of the same. The event proved to be a massive crush, and Mira wondered how she was expected to spot anyone at all whatsoever. Still, as she was led on George's arm to meet her host and hostess, Mira searched for Harry as diligently as she dared.

"Keeping an eye out for Lord Haversham, are you?" George observed.

Surprised at his acuity, Mira felt at a loss for a reply.

"You won't find him here," he added.

"Why ever not?" Mira demanded. "He is as likely to have been invited to this event as you and I."

"True," George said shortly. "Is that not his mother languishing on the arm of her gallant husband just this side of the fireplace?"

Mira managed to spot Lord and Lady Avery in spite of not equaling George's height. "Certainly with his parents in attendance, there is no reason why he should not be also," she said in a tone of voice designed to hide her burgeoning delight.

"Ah, but the tiger and the cub are not created equal," George mused as he took a glass of champagne from the platter of a passing footman.

Mira drew her arm from that of her escort and refused to take another step with him. "By that I suppose you mean that Viscount Haversham is inferior to his father, the Earl of Avery?"

"Not at all! I only meant that *Bertie*, as he insists on being called, has better things with which to occupy himself."

Mira felt crushed. Harry *did* have better things to do. Hadn't he told her as much? And she hadn't believed him. "George, what do you mean? You must tell me!"

"I must?" he drawled. "Only it would seem I have better things to do as well."

Mira watched in disbelief as her self-imposed future husband turned on his heel and walked away. Her mother and brothers were nowhere to be seen so she counted it a blessing when Lord and Lady Avery approached, the Countess's hands poised for clapping.

"My darling girl!" Lady Avery gushed. "How good it is to see you with your hair up and your skirts let down at last! If only Herbert were here to see you. I know he would bespeak every dance. Don't you think so, my beloved?" she asked, turning to her husband.

"Yes, my flower, she is almost as lovely as yourself when you were of an age."

"Oh, Eustace," Lady Avery said with a bat of her fan to his arm. "You make it sound as if I were nearly old enough to be her mother!" The fact that she was possessed of a son three years older than Mira seemed to utterly escape the Countess.

"Lady Avery, I am so pleased to see you as well. Is Bertie to join us tonight?" Mira asked whilst congratulating herself on having remembered to use Harry's new name. "There was something I most particularly wished to discuss with him."

"Bertie who?" Lord Avery asked.

Mira wondered if perhaps he were poking fun at his son, but he seemed genuinely baffled. "I do beg your pardon!" Mira amended. "It is Harry of whom I speak."

"Oh! Is Herbert in town?" Lady Avery asked, her eyebrows shooting up in surprise so far as to disappear under her preposterous turban. She turned to her husband who, as always, waited patiently at her elbow in the case he would be needed to assist his wife or, more often than not, counter the effects of her actions on her surroundings.

"Yes, my love, do you not recall? His request for permission to attend the Crenshaws on their journey was prettily done, if I do say so myself," Lord Avery remarked.

"Well, if you shan't, Eustace, who shall?" With that puzzling observation, Lady Avery returned her attention to Mira, her lips a thin line of disapproval. "Where, then, is my son? I suppose you believe you can keep him from me, but for how long? Eventually he will need to eat and to sleep and . . . and . . .: she continued, a wild look in her eye, "and to read the newspaper! When he does, it will be at my door he is scratching, I tell you!"

Mira, somewhat acquainted with Lady Avery's fits and starts, refused to be led down the garden path by such spurious conversation. "I most humbly beg your pardon," Mira ventured, "but Harry left us this morning." She wisely chose to leave out the information that Harry hadn't actually joined them until midway through their journey. "We haven't seen him since. I was rather hoping you might tell me where he is."

"In that case," Lady Avery cooed as if there had not been a cross word between them, "he should be here at any moment. Of this I am most certain. He would not wish to miss your very first ball, my darling girl!"

But Harry did not come.

chapter eight

The second morning since his arrival in London, Harry stood on the step of Haversham House, feeling as if he were embarking on his execution rather than an audience with his mother. He was glumly aware he had been expected a forty-eight hours prior, and the mere three hours of sleep he had enjoyed after his adventure at the Pagoda did nothing to improve his outlook. He hoped his mother would be in one of her sunnier moods; the road ahead would be difficult enough, even with her cooperation.

As he hadn't a key, he was forced to ring the bell, a circumstance which meant his mother would be alerted as to the presence of a guest. This would make it impossible for him to submit to the temptation to duck into his own chamber in order to catch up on his sleep. The missing paper must be obtained from George before nightfall, however, and Harry needed his mother's help in so doing.

"Herbert!" his mother cried when he appeared at her side, his expression appropriately chastened and apologies on the tip of his tongue. "Have you any idea how anxious I have been?" she cried.

Harry looked about and noted a bowl containing water and a wet cloth, a variety of elixir bottles displayed amongst the bibelot on the sofa table, and more than the usual number of pillows arranged under his mother's head which was topped with a lace cap, absurdly askew.

"I can see my absence has caused you considerable distress," he soothed as he plumped the pillows, tidied the bottles, and rang for the butler to bring a fresh cloth and bowl of water. "However, I was not at liberty to come to you before now and as I had no idea as to when I might be able to wait on you, I felt it best to remain silent until I might bring you the news in person," he said in a light voice designed to distract her from his negligence.

"News of what, Herbert?" Lady Avery asked, her face alight with pleasure at the promise of a delicious *on dit.*

"The news of my arrival, of course." He stepped to the fireplace and feigned an interest in the mantle clock so that his mother did not witness his own apprehension.

"Oh, yes!" Lady Avery cried with a clap of her hands, an occurrence so frequent Harry often wondered why her hands didn't simply give up the ghost and snap off at the wrists. "I have been waiting for you ever so long! It wouldn't have been so dreadful except the Crenshaw girl insisted you left for London in train with her family *weeks* ago!"

"You spoke with Mira?" he asked, secretly hoping his mother didn't notice how his head swerved around at mention of his beloved's name.

"Of course! At the Wellborns' ball. She was there with that cousin of hers, Forge or Porgy or . . ."

"George," Harry supplied.

"Yes! George! I can never remember it; it's such a foreign-sounding name!"

"It was the name of our last four kings," Harry said dryly.

"Yes, I suppose that's true," she said in a faint voice.

"Now, Mother, don't you go under on me. I need you!"

"You need me?" She sat up, suddenly full of vim and vigor. "For what? And what can you possibly mean about my going under? I will have you know, I don't go under!"

"But of course you do," Harry said, sitting down next to her on the sofa. "It is one of your most tenacious charms. Now," he said, holding up a hand to ward off further questions, "before I become distracted by your numerous other tenacious qualities, I find I have a problem, one with which you might help."

"Oh, Herbert, does it have anything to do with those special letters you were receiving at the Abbey?"

"Yes, dearest, how utterly perceptive of you! You haven't said anything to Father about them, have you?"

"No, Herbert, I gave my word," she breathed.

"Speaking of which, he is not due home any moment, is he?"

Lady Avery collapsed against the sofa cushions and let out a sigh of exasperation. "*Mais non*! He would remain at his club all the day long if there were nothing to prevent it."

"In that case, what would prevent him?" Harry asked.

"Prevent who, what?" she asked, her face an utter blank.

"Father. Might he stay at his club all day today or is there something to prevent him?" Harry said with what remained of his store of patience.

"Well, *I* would prevent him if I could!"

"What I need to know is have you? Prevented him? From staying at his club all day today?"

"As if he would listen to a thing I have to say, Herbert!" Lady Avery replied in her most disagreeable tones. "Really, you do try my patience!"

Harry drew a deep sigh and took her hands in his. "What I meant to ask is: are we quite alone?"

Lady Avery conducted an exaggerated visual tour of the room. "Do you see anyone, my darling?"

"No, I don't, but your butler has been known to put a glass to the wall and not infrequently, I might add."

"Yes, dear, but he has grown quite deaf and one glass won't do. I suppose he could try two but I'm not sure how he would work it out exactly," Lady Avery said, her brow furrowed with pointless concentration.

"Very well. I need you to pay the strictest attention to what I say. Can you do that?" Harry asked with hopes he did not sound as condescending as he felt.

"I suppose so. I can be quite perspicacious when I wish to be. Perspicacious—what a lovely word! I don't believe I've used it before," Lady Avery mused.

"I believe you must have a different word in mind. Perspicacious means to be shrewd and quick-witted."

"Yes, exactly!" Lady Avery cried with a vehement nod of her head.

"Well then," Harry said in hopes he had adequately stifled his astonishment, "let us hope you are correct for the task I require of you shall require much quick thinking indeed. I shall need you to throw a party. A large one. Tonight." He fought the urge to turn away so as to spare himself the sight of his mother's reaction but allowed himself an internal wince and braced for the worst.

"But Herbert! How can I?" she said in a languid manner quite opposite to the one he had expected. "You know I am always the last of the better families to give their annual ball.

Everything is all set for the end of the Season. So you see there is nothing to be done."

"But, dearest, I need to run into a certain gentleman, and it must look unintentional. I can think of no other way to accomplish it."

"Tonight! Did you say tonight?" she exclaimed as if the meaning of his request had only now been comprehended. "I can't possibly! How am I to know how to out-do my friends if I don't hold my do last?" she implored, jumping to her feet and pulling at her hair. "And how can I be the first to hold her do right after the Wellborns' spectacular do? They had live fish swimming in the stream arranged down the center of the head table. Live fish! The only other person known to do such a thing was Prinny himself. Now that he is dead I suppose it is perfectly justified to ape his fashions, but where am I to get live fish by tonight? And twice as many? And they must be bigger and more beautifully colored, and I will quite simply *die* if I don't have live fish swimming at table for my party!"

"Mama, please do not take on so," Harry soothed, realizing that he had set about a far more onerous task than he had supposed. "I now perceive how difficult it would be for you to do as I have requested. I will find another way. I suppose Lady Crenshaw would be willing to attempt it for me."

"Lady Crenshaw? Where is *she* to find live fish by this evening?"

"Well," Harry wheedled with a sudden spurt of inspiration. "I am persuaded she could manage it. However, if she does, I am fairly sure everyone will make her an object of fun."

"Whatever for?" Lady Avery demanded. "Aside from that ghastly turban she has worn these last two seasons."

"I think it would be obvious to everyone that she was merely attempting to out-do the Wellborns, and I highly doubt she should come out on the sunny side of that comparison."

Lady Avery collapsed onto the sofa as understanding dawned. "Why, Herbert, you are so very clever! I could pull it off, absolutely, but Lady Crenshaw would surely have much to apologize for should she make the attempt. But I think I shall not," she mused in so mysterious a fashion, Harry couldn't be sure of her intentions.

"So Lady Crenshaw should be cannon fodder for the elite of London society?"

"No, of course not, Herbert! I shall give the party but I shan't attempt to out-do the Wellborns. People will be expecting it, of course! Can you not see the tears of boredom starting in my eyes already?" she demanded.

"Yes, Mother, and they are quite unbecoming. To not attempt something far more ravishing than the Wellborns' do is a devastating thought, but I think you have hit on something quite unique."

"Why darling boy, what can you mean?"

"Why, you said it yourself, not a moment ago! Everyone will be expecting you to throw a lavish party and will never allow it to be better than, or even as good, as the Wellborns' do, so why not go a hundred miles in the opposite direction and throw a party that is as understated as it is elegant?" Harry suggested, silently congratulating himself on his own perspicacity.

"But of course!" Lady Avery declared and followed it with a round of applause. "I shall bedeck the tables and chairs with ivy from the square, for, as I am forever saying, one can't possibly be more understated than when one is forced to pick offerings from the garden."

"I do believe I have heard you say so on more than one occasion," Harry said, assuring himself it wasn't a lie if you uttered it for the sake of one's country.

"But Herbert, do you think it elegant enough?"

"Ivy has a classical air about it. What could be more elegant than that which calls to mind Helen of Troy or Diana the Huntress?"

"My thoughts exactly!" Lady Avery replied with a smile of pure delight. "I shall wear my Greek Key gown that I have had, oh . . . even before Porgy the Sixth was king."

"George the Fourth," Harry corrected.

His mother had the grace to look struck. "I suppose it only *seemed* as if there were six of them. I declare, every time I look around, there is a new George about to be crowned."

Harry deemed it unwise to point out that his mother had been born only long enough to witness the crowning of a single George and pressed on. "What about food? Have you any in the house?"

Lady Avery looked down her nose at her son. "Of course we have! What are we to eat if not food?"

"But, is there enough to feed all of your guests or should you take out the carriage and bespeak yourself a feast?"

"Oh, yes, I see. Though the cheese and apple slices we brought along from the Abbey are certainly understated, they are hardly elegant."

"Mama, I do believe you are perspicacious after all. Do be a dear and take yourself upstairs to smarten yourself up a bit. Perhaps a bonnet that promises to cover that crooked cap of yours. Meanwhile, I shall write out invitations. How does that sound?"

"It sounds wonderful, Herbert!" Lady Avery cried with nary a clap as she rushed to her room for her cloak and bonnet.

Harry pulled the bell for Webster to bespeak paper and pen when it suddenly occurred to him that the old servant had never appeared when Harry had rung for him ten minutes prior. Perhaps he has been listening through the wall after all. However, when the butler appeared, he seemed very much his usual self and claimed not to have heard the earlier ring.

Nevertheless, Harry fretted over the matter of Webster as he waited for the promised articles to arrive but forced his fears aside in order to write out invitations. It was more than a little unusual to invite people to a party with only a few hours' notice, but Harry was determined. In order to assuage any suspicions George might develop, Harry wrote a note that indicated this was a secondary invitation as no response to the first had been received. As for the remainder of the guests, he knew they were accustomed to his mother's flights of fancy and forged on with hopes that most would be curious enough to cast aside their previous plans for the evening in favor of the ball at Haversham House.

In truth, the only guest he required the attendance of was George, but that would never do. Harry must somehow create a situation in which he could discover the whereabouts of his orders and be off to collect them whilst George was otherwise occupied. That required a crowd. Lord and Lady Crenshaw and family were invited which would serve as an excellent diversion for George.

It would also give Harry the opportunity to see Mira and possibly dance with her close enough in his arms that he could discover what it was that had so drastically changed her attitude the last time he had seen her. Harry would give up his duties as a secret service agent in an instant if it meant Mira could be his, except for one thing—the life of the Queen. He must find out what was in those orders and as soon as possible.

By the time Lady Avery returned, Harry had completed his chore. He would divide the missives amongst the footmen to deliver, but he would hand carry those addressed to the Duke of Marcross and the Crenshaws. He allowed himself only enough time to buss his mother on the cheek on his way out the door, jumped into his waiting carriage, and tooled his way as speedily as he dared to the houses Crenshaw, home to George and his mother whilst in London, and Wembley, the townhouse owned by Mira's father.

He had hoped for a glimpse of Mira when the door opened, but not a soul save the footman who answered his knock was to be seen. Disappointed, Harry returned to his conveyance but hesitated to drive away. He wished to ensure Mira would attend and hoped for some sign that he was not so thoroughly in her black books that she would refuse. He was rewarded for his patience when, a few moments later, there appeared a pale oval encircled by red curls at one of the upper story windows.

Harry wished to leap to his feet and wave his hat in the air but decided Mira would deem it too Bertie-like. Instead, he chose to favor her with a more restrained inclination of the head followed by the most speaking look he could manage at such a distance. When she opened the window and smiled down at him, he limited himself to a mere smile in return. Then, with a sense of well-being he had not enjoyed for quite some time, he turned his carriage in the direction of Haversham House in order to prepare a toilette that bespoke enough of Bertie to maintain his alter ego and enough of his true self to best please Mira.

However, when he arrived back at Haversham House, he was dismayed to find matters in total disarray. The front of the house crawled with footman who hacked away at the shrubbery. Inside, the house was overrun with people who scurried to and fro with platters of food, pieces of silver, enormous baskets of flowers, and more than a few who were each in possession of a six-foot statue.

"Mother!" he shouted as he ran up the stairs to accost his parent, but she was nowhere to be found. Instead, he discovered the drawing room had been pillaged of its furniture and its walls lined with a row of stone plinths, most of which bore a statue classical in nature, while the far end of the room sported an arrangement of a huge wicker birdcage supported by several birdbaths of stone surrounded by potted ferns. "Did we not agree on understated?" Harry demanded of no one in particular.

As there was little time remaining before dinner, a meal he decided to take in his room in light of the chaos below, Harry cast aside concerns for the party and turned his thoughts to his task for the evening. He pulled aside a harried-looking footman, ordered up hot water for his bath, and went straight to his clothespress to ensure suitable evening attire awaited, fully aware that his mother had insisted on ordering a new wardrobe for his use every year in spite of his lack of return.

His measurements had altered a bit over the past four years but not in the waist, he was gratified to learn, and not so much in the chest that he couldn't fasten his coat. As much as he longed to banish Bertie for the evening, he knew he dared not. Nevertheless, he recklessly eschewed the use of lace at collar or wrists and owned it felt good to dress like a man. He hoped it pleased Mira as much as it pleased himself.

He planned his strategy over his dinner tray which consisted of watered-down broth, hastily assembled cucumber sandwiches, a rice pudding and, predictably, sliced apples and cheese, all of which were sure to be on the menu for the party as well. "I thought we agreed on elegant," he mumbled into his spoon, then chided himself for his critique. It hardly mattered what was served; the retrieval of his orders was the only item on the menu for the night.

As he made his way back to the drawing room he congratulated himself on his accomplishments thus far: he had arranged for an opportunity to meet up with George under favorable conditions, he had kept his mother's thoughts occupied with party preparations rather than the reasons behind Harry's request, and he had managed to elicit a smile from Mira. So far, matters had moved forward quite satisfactorily.

With a veritable song in his heart, Harry pulled open the drawing room doors and was assaulted with the most bizarre sight of his entire life. His mother stood barefoot and posed on a plinth at the far end of the room swathed in a too-small Grecian robe and a thoroughly modern feathered turban on her head. However, it was that every visible inch of her face and body was caked with what looked, remarkably, like mud from the garden that took Harry most by surprise.

"Herbert!" Lady Avery cried through a mouth rendered nearly immobile by the thick, dry layer of stuff she had smeared all over her face, neck, and arms. She began to babble at length, but Harry only caught one word in ten. Clearly the preservation of her creation, already cracked in the corners of her lips and becoming more compromised with every word, was of a higher priority than comprehension. However, Harry thought he knew what it was she would have him know.

"Thank you, Mother. I *am* pleased to have found an evening suit that fits so well. Which brings to mind the close fit of whatever it is you are, er, wearing. And *do* please relax your arms. It is a charming attitude you have struck but it looks deuced uncomfortable, not to mention that bits and pieces of, er . . . are sloughing off at an alarming rate and lodging in your décolletage."

His mother let her arms fall to her sides in defeat. "I thought it would please you! I only wished to coordinate with my understated and elegant décor."

"In that case, would it be too rude to query as to what prompted the turban? Wouldn't a wreath of ivy be more in keeping with the theme?"

"You are right, of course, my darling, but do you not recall what I said earlier about Lady Crenshaw's turban? It is tedious beyond words so I have long been determined to wear this delightful one when next I entertained. As a leader of fashion, I must take my responsibilities seriously," she explained as a large chunk of dried sludge slid off the side of her face and hit the stone plinth with a low thunk.

"But, Mother, that isn't mud, is it? From the garden?"

"Yes," she hissed through the weight on her lips. "What else?"

Stunned, Harry could only stare in fascinated horror as his mother once again took up her awkward pose of one knee drawn up and arms raised in supplication to the gods above. Harry had to own it was naïve of him to expect an evening devoid of his mother's feather-brained antics and thanked the Lord for small favors when he noted that her mud-smeared palms would surely prevent her from clapping, at least until it had dried, cracked, and joined its fellows in the folds of the Greek robe.

He had imagined that he and his mother would greet their guests as they stood, side-by-elegant-side, in the drawing room where there would be conversation and dancing. However, as he had no plinth of his own, he made his way to the front hall to greet his guests as they entered the house. He hated to appear too eager in the eyes of George, as well as those of Mira, but it was difficult to find too much fault with such an insouciant approach when one considered the alternative. Harry reminded himself that it was meant to be a casual affair after all, and with a deep breath, he girded up his loins for the evening ahead.

chapter nine

Mira was pleased with one thing; she was to be escorted to the Avery's party by her parents and brothers and not the tedious George. She was very glad of another; the hoped-for opportunity to dance with Harry in order to beg his pardon for her behavior last time they had met. She was puzzled as to why she had not seen him in London before now but owned that it was very sweet of Harry to hand deliver her invitation. It was with great relief that she realized he was not angry with her.

Though she had spent two entire Harry-free days in London, they were not hours spent in idleness. She had greatly enjoyed taking her bows in the presence of the young and beautiful Queen Victoria the day after their arrival in London, and Mira felt both intimidated and awe-inspired when she considered that she was a mere few years younger than the monarch. Mira and her mother had also spent a goodly amount of time in the shops and had ordered many new gowns to be done up. Now that she was in the city, Mira could see that some of her fashions were a bit young and did not convey the aura of sophistication she hoped to exude. Her mother no doubt thought her shockingly wasteful, but her father, a man of exquisite tastes, insisted Mira was correct and new gowns should be had.

As she submitted to being turned and pinned and turned again by the dressmaker, Mira realized she had intuitively chosen her previous gowns based on the Harry she had once known. The Harry she had met since was far more dashing than she had ever imagined, and she feared he would look down his nose on a plethora of rosebuds, lace, and knotted ribbon. Instead, she chose more subdued fashions that were the crack of fashion, a bit more off the shoulder, with less pronounced puffed sleeves, and in sumptuous fabrics that accentuated her silhouette rather than obscured it.

It would be weeks before most of the new gowns would be ready, but she had insisted that her favorite, a ball gown of silver tissue with a pink silk rose at the waist, be done up right away. Of this she was most glad of all for it had been delivered just in time for Mira to don it for the Avery's last minute party at Haversham House. Together with a silver ribbon for her hair, short lace gloves, and pink square-toed dancing slippers, she felt ready for most anything.

She reached the front hall just as her parents strolled in from the library, her papa's eyes lighting up when he saw her. "Now, that is worth any amount of money!" he said, taking his daughter's hand and twirling her about.

"I am so very glad you like it, Papa, but I am afraid you shall be sadly shocked when you are dunned for it," Mira admitted.

Lord Crenshaw looked a question at his wife who merely shook her head and turned away.

"I say, you do look stunning!" Adrian said as he descended the stairs with Stephen close on his heels.

"I agree," Stephen chimed. "Meanwhile, Mira, you should know that a gathering at Haversham House always includes a few surprises. It is best to behave as if you don't notice."

"Notice what?" Mira asked, alarmed.

"Lady Avery. Entirely," Adrian said dryly.

"You can't be serious! I am to ignore my hostess?" Mira demanded.

"It's best," Stephen added with a nod.

"Stop exaggerating, you two," Lady Crenshaw sang out. "Of course you are not to ignore Lady Avery, Mira. Your manners, as always, should be impeccable. However, your brothers are correct in that you should take no notice of her little oddities."

"Little oddities?" Mira echoed. "How little? Am I likely to ignore them unnoticed?"

"Nothing little about 'em," Adrian insisted. "However, as everyone else will be doing the selfsame thing, you needn't feel as if you are risking social censure by looking the other way."

Mira felt her tension dissolve. "Oh, I see! I believe I can do that. But, truly, what sort of little oddities should I be expecting? I am already most familiar with the hand-clapping," she added.

"The hand-clapping is, without a doubt, the most annoying, but it is rather a small one in comparison to some of the antics I've seen," Stephen replied.

"Now, boys," their mother admonished as she pulled on her gloves and checked her appearance in the pier glass in the front hall.

"No, Mama, we must speak," Adrian said. "It's hardly fair to Mira, otherwise."

I have to say I agree with Adrian," Sir Anthony pointed out, standing next to his wife in the mirror and examining her appearance as well. "Ravishing, as always, my dear!" he said with a peck to her cheek.

Lady Crenshaw heaved a deep sigh which Adrian took as capitulation and opened his budget on all things Lady Avery. "There was the time she threw a masquerade ball and she dressed as Boudicca. She carried off more than one woman's wig with her spear, I must say! And as for the men, they were in constant danger of having their eyes put out."

"I was never so glad I dressed as a pirate that year," Sir Anthony mused.

"One eye patch was not sufficient for our esteemed father," Adrian said in mocking tones.

"Adrian, my boy, you must admit that a firm defense was warranted even if the sightless state does not mix well with waltzing," his father intoned.

Stephen laughed. "It was indeed hazardous," he insisted. "But that was not the worst. Do you not remember the ball at which she wore those shocking shoes! I don't know how she managed to convince anyone to make them for her; they were downright dangerous!"

"Dangerous? Why?" Mira asked, almost afraid of the answer.

"They were ordinary enough shoes," Adrian explained, "but she browbeat some poor soul into attaching them to blocks of wood because she wished to be the tallest lady in attendance. She continually fell off of them to land in a heap on the floor until the gentleman caught on and felt obliged to catch her in their arms. It put more than one lady's nose out of joint that night," he said with a shake of his head.

"That was not the worst by a long shot!" Stephen shuddered. "It was the musical evening she hosted."

"What's wrong with a musical evening? It sounds lovely," Mira replied in hopes she did not sound as defensive as she felt. They were referring to Harry's mother after all.

"Music is fairly tolerable," Stephen admitted, "but this was opera, and Lady Avery insisted on singing."

"Oh!" Mira exclaimed, delighted. "I hadn't known Lady Avery could sing!

"She can't," Lady Crenshaw murmured under her breath, then pretended she hadn't spoken.

"Not a note," Stephen continued. "She hit every single one of them wrong and most of the words as well, not to mention, her Italian is execrable."

"Oh, poor Harry!" Mira said. "That must have been dreadful for him."

"Don't you mean *Bertie*?" Stephen asked mockingly. "At any rate, he wasn't there. We were none of us old enough to attend any of her parties until after he had left for the Continent. I'm afraid he's in for a bit of a nasty shock tonight."

"My favorite is the one how Lord Avery caught his hair on fire whilst reciting some appalling poetry," Adrian said, "but I can't think that one possibly true."

"Let me assure you, Mira," Sir Anthony added with a wag of his finger, "it is all true, every soul-quaking word of it. Hair erupting into flame, tiny dogs bursting from bosoms, ghosts in the cemetery, all of it! Now, it is time to be off to discover whatever new horror awaits us."

"Oh, Anthony, you know it's not as bad as you make it out to be," his wife said with a bat of her fan to his arm as they disappeared through the open door.

Mira, a brother on each arm as they took the flight of steps to the street where their carriage awaited, dared to continue the conversation. "Why haven't you two ever spoken of this before?" she asked in whispered tones.

"We thought you most likely to end up with her as a mama-in-law and we didn't want to discourage it," Adrian explained.

"But now you don't mind if I am discouraged?"

"We're counting on it," Stephen drawled.

Mira felt her spine stiffen. "I rather like Lady Avery, and I know she likes me. Perhaps we would get on famously were I to become Harry's wife."

"Not in the least likely," Stephen shot back.

"Which, getting along with Lady Avery or marrying Harry?" Mira asked.

"Harry who?" Adrian scoffed and handed her into the carriage.

As Mira rode to Haversham Hall with her family, she began to doubt it had been best to warn her of what to expect. She could feel the strain rise higher and higher with every passing moment until she thought perhaps her hair was standing on end. Indeed, it was a shame as she felt sure Harry would ensure he wouldn't allow his mother to behave in such a fashion. Her brothers had indicated that Harry had not been in attendance when these appalling incidents occurred, a thought that certainly explained everything. Lord Avery was too easily blown over by his wife's merest whim, but Harry would make sure matters went smoothly when he was present.

Feeling slightly mollified, Mira gazed out the window as the lights from row after row of lovely Georgian townhouses flashed by. It was a treat when everyone in the neighborhood was in town for the Season and each home occupied and full of life. Haversham House was not far, and it wasn't long before the lights of that particular manse filled the night sky.

Indeed, there was so much light Mira wondered that it could not be seen from the upper windows of her own home. Every pane of glass was ablaze, though it was clear most of the rooms were not occupied, and the walkway in front of the house was lined with numerous flambeaux of alarming height. As they waited their turn to disembark, Mira could not keep her eyes from the torches, sure that one of the guests would be engulfed in flames unawares, or, at the very least, overcome with smoke.

"What on God's green earth . . ." Sir Anthony barked as he pushed past Mira to have a better look out of the window. "Ladies, leave your cloaks in the carriage, and it would be wise to crumple those balls of puff you call sleeves as you pass by those torches."

"He's simply envious that those puffs never caught on amongst the masculine set," Adrian said with a wink for his sister.

Mira laughed and felt grateful for her family, while, at the same time, sad that this tight-knit, little group would one day be separated, for what was this Season in London about if not her marriage? When her brothers married, their wives would join the family of which Mira was now a part. When she married, she would join her husband's family. Though she would not live with her parents should she marry George, she would still be a Crenshaw. There was some comfort in that but little else. Mira found of late that George made her flesh crawl, whilst Harry made the blood sing in her veins. She hoped to dance with many gentlemen tonight for one reason and one reason only: to be made more attractive in the eyes of he whom she most admired.

The five of them made their way out of the carriage and walked along, one at a time, as the paving did not allow for even two abreast without danger of bursting into flame. As it happened, Mira was the last to enter the portals of Haversham Hall and was more than a little surprised by the way Harry's face flooded with relief when he saw her.

"Miss Crenshaw," he blurted out in full Bertie-like glory, "it is so good, yes, *so* good to see you! What an honor that you have chosen to attend our little do over the dozens of invitations you must have received for tonight."

Mira saw how her brother's faces fell, but she was not fooled. The emergence of Bertie was something Harry felt necessary, though she had no idea why. Meanwhile, she was much more impressed by his very natty attire of black suit and waistcoat over a crisp white shirt devoid of even a scrap of lace. He wore a single fob, the attached watch tucked into its pocket, and a diamond pin in his cravat. The lack of color accentuated the green of his eyes and the touch of sun in his cheeks, while it brought out the yellow of his hair. Mira thought she had never seen him look more handsome.

"None other offered such promise," she replied with expectations that she would receive no other evidence of his pleasure at her presence until later in the evening. However, in that she was happily wrong and was thrilled when he took her hand and allowed his lips to hover over it a bit longer than necessary.

"Save a waltz for me," he whispered with a puff of warm air that made its way through Mira's glove to her skin. She gave her consent with a squeeze of his fingers in her own and moved away to join her parents as they made their ascent up the stairs to the drawing room.

"It is passing strange that this house is not possessed of a ballroom," Lady Crenshaw mused.

"Oh, it is," Stephen said. "Har . . . that is, Bertie and I have spent many an afternoon in it playing at cricket, bowling, and archery."

"Who knew his parents would have ever allowed him anything as dangerous as a bow and arrow?" Sir Anthony quizzed.

"They didn't. He filched it," Stephen said.

"He never did!" Mira cried. "He wouldn't!"

"You would be surprised at some of the things he has done, Mira," Adrian said, his expression dark.

"Adrian and Stephen," Lady Crenshaw said, *sotto voce.* "You betray your friend when you speak of him thus."

Mira felt foreboding clutch her chest but knew it would do her little good to ask impertinent questions. Fortunately, they progressed only a few more steps up the crowded staircase before Stephen ventured a response. "I merely feel that Mira should have the truth. She speaks of him as if he were some kind of saint, which he very much is not," he said with a snort.

"I know he isn't," Mira riposted but she had to own she knew very little of Harry that would style him as wicked other than the gun she had seen on his person. In addition, she hated that he had lied to her and refused to tell her the truth even whilst admiring how he remained firm in his principles and admitting that the aura of danger he had recently acquired in her eyes made him infinitely more attractive.

Then she recalled something her brothers had spoken of the other day. "Do you refer to the boating accident?" she asked, but the crowd was heavy and hot, the stairs treacherous to traverse, and no one paid her the slightest heed. She made a mental note to ask Harry himself later when they waltzed in each other's arms.

It took an unconscionable amount of time to reach the top of the stairs and the doors of the drawing room. However, Mira doubted there was a soul present who regretted the wait, for she stepped into the room just in time to witness how a gentleman in military red unwittingly snagged with his dress sword the hem of Lady Avery's Greek Key robe. It was just what was needed for the punished seams of the too-small gown to give way altogether and collapse in snowy folds at her feet.

At the same time, there came a commotion from the floor below. It seemed a guest had entered the house and was so eager to reach the festivities that he pushed his way up the stairs, a circumstance that caused more than one guest to stumble with shrieks of dismay. As he stormed across the hall and threw open the doors, Lady Avery screamed with alarm and shouted, "Oh, Eustace, it is exactly like the Rape of the Sabine Women!" whereupon she collapsed gracefully into a pile of white silk and dried mud.

"My petal!" cried the newcomer, and with three long strides, he was at her side. Mira was amused to see how the men fell back and the women pressed forward to witness the scene. She was no exception and was vastly relieved to find that Lady Avery was entirely covered in the muddy substance that shielded her from almost utter nakedness. She was also glad to see that the guest who had burst on the scene was none other than Lord Avery and that he had the situation well in hand. It was clear he relished his role as rescuer as he whipped off his coat in a frenzy to protect his wife from prying eyes.

"There there, my love, did we not discuss how inadvisable it is for you to entertain without my knowledge?" He drew her towards the door, the crowd most pleased to give them a wide berth.

"Yes, Eustace, you have said so on many occasions, but Herbert asked if I would not throw him a party, and I could not say him nay," she wailed as the dried mud cascaded from her skin like a shower of dying stars. "I so wanted to prove that I could be understated as well as elegant!"

"Understated, my foot!" exclaimed a woman with a formidable amount of gray hair piled high on her head and held in place with a garish enameled pin. She gave a tsk and turned away.

"If it weren't for such scenes, I would never attend her parties," another woman remarked to her neighbor, and they, too, turned their backs on the Averys as they made their humiliating progress across the room.

By the time Lord and Lady Avery had neared the door, every single one of the guests had cut dead their hostess with the exception of Mira and her mother who took Lady Avery's free arm and went with them. At the landing they met their son as he obtained the top of the stairs. Mira could not fathom what he was thinking. His face was as inscrutable as a night with no moon, and he remained entirely silent as he followed his parents up the next set of stairs to their private rooms.

Mira hardly knew where to look. She burned with shame exactly as if she were the one whose gown had fallen in a puddle at her feet. She wondered if further disasters such as this were something she had to look forward to if she married Harry, for he had been present and catastrophe had not been averted as she had supposed. Worst of all, she wondered if enduring such social debacles on a regular basis would cause her to blame Harry or think less of him, or, even, love him less.

These were sobering thoughts indeed. When she felt a touch at her elbow and turned to see Harry, his face set in rigid lines even while his eyes beseeched her, Mira's heart quaked within her.

"Harry, ..." she began but could think of not one thing to say that would address both his pride and his pain all at once. The necessity of a cogent reply was made pointless when he dropped his gaze to the floor, executed a deep bow, and strode away. When he instructed the orchestra to play, and the strains of a waltz filled the room, she began to move towards him, determined to find the right words as they danced, but was brought up short when Harry stepped up to Lucy Sutherland and waltzed off with her in his arms.

Mira felt as if she had been slapped in the face. Lucy's coy behavior towards Harry as they danced did nothing to mellow Mira's feelings. A kind and genial girl, Lucy, if one were to judge by the alarming frequency with which she batted her lashes and wielded her fan, appeared to have had her head turned by the invitation to partner her host for the opening dance.

Mira, resolved to appear as if she hadn't noticed and, furthermore, shouldn't care a farthing if she had, joined a cluster of women in conversation but could not refrain from monitoring the proceedings from the corner of her eye.

When Lucy leaned in too close, quite purposefully brushing her bosom against Harry as he made some remark, Mira felt her own bosom heave with indignation. When Lucy emitted a trill of delight, Mira wished for nothing more than the opportunity to thrust her fan down the raven-haired beauty's throat, the one with the fetching mole set against skin of alabaster white. When the music stopped, and Lucy joined Harry in a promenade about the room and twisted a glossy ringlet around and around her finger whilst giving him an arch smile, Mira nearly choked on the apple slice she had forced into her mouth.

Finally, music for the March began, and Mira was gratified when George entered the room and lost no time in claiming her hand for the dance. "I thought you would never arrive," Mira said in a voice designed to rise gracefully above the music and into Harry's ears.

George lifted a brow in surprise. "I am fortunate to find you unengaged. I had thought, surely, you would be on the dance floor this far advanced in the evening."

"There was a bit of a *contretemps* tonight, and it delayed things," Mira said, taking his proffered hand and all but dragging him onto the dance floor. "But all is well now.

"Of course," George replied in a wry voice. "One might always count on a *contretemps* at an Avery event."

Mira wanted to skewer him with her fan, but instead risked a glance at Harry who danced close enough to catch George's remark. Harry, his jaw tight with tension, gave no other sign he had overheard the insult and bent his full attention on his partner who, to Mira's annoyance, was once again the besotted Lucy.

The March seemed to go on forever. The fact that George was an admirable dancer, almost as skilled as Mira, did nothing to further her enjoyment. Try as she might, her gaze would stray over and over again to Harry and Lucy, and Mira was struck each time by how well they looked together. Lucy's black hair and eyes and snow-white complexion were the perfect foil to Harry's golden coloring, and it was clear that others in the room had noticed the same, the least of which was far from Lucy's mother who blushed and nodded constantly as well wishers paid their compliments on her well-favored daughter. With a sigh, Mira tried to remember why it was she had been so eager to attend.

She was never so glad when a dance came to an end and looked forward to a rest when Harry caught her eye, made his bows to Lucy, and made his way to Mira's side.

"I was hoping we might speak in private."

"Of course, I was wishful of the same," Mira said in a rush, as if he would walk away again if she wasn't entirely clear that she wanted nothing more than to be with him.

"My apologies, Miss Crenshaw, I mean no disrespect, but I was addressing the Duke."

She had forgotten that George still stood at her side, and, for the second time that evening, Mira was robbed of words. Why on earth should Harry wish to speak to George? She felt that something was quite wrong, and then there came a stir from the far end of the room. Lady Avery, adorned in a gold gown bearing puffed sleeves so large she was forced to hold her arms out at her sides, entered, remounted her plinth, and announced in a voice that sounded very much like doom: "I have returned."

chapter ten

Harry was aghast. Why hadn't his father kept his mother confined to her rooms? Surely one fit of fainting and nudity was enough for anyone's evening. He wanted to drop his head into his hands; he yearned to sink into the floor; he wished his *mother* to sink into the floor, but, in spite of the intensity of his desires, none of these things transpired. After a moment of stunned silence, all returned to what had been: the orchestra resumed its melody, the couples returned to their dance, and Harry stood, stock still and silent, quite incapable of summoning a Bertie-like chuckle or *bon mots* to save his life.

The expression on George's face proved that he thoroughly enjoyed Harry's plight, but it was Mira's reaction that undid him. She looked a question at him, her magnificent blue eyes sparkling with tears, and when he would not, or rather, could not, speak, she gave him a tremulous smile and walked away. Harry should have been glad of this chance to speak to George alone but knew his voice would betray him. Instead, he watched, his throat aching, as Mira approached his mother.

"Lady Avery," she said, brightly. "Your gown is stunning! Wherever did you have it made? I must be sure to patronize her shop the next time I am in need of something quite this spectacular."

"Oh, Miss Crenshaw!" his mother cried, bending towards Mira and clapping her hands.

Harry admired the deftness with which Mira dipped in order to avoid being clouted in the head with an enormous sleeve. He admired her sapphire blue eyes and the variety of colors that made up her fiery hair. He admired her kindness to his mother and longed to tell her so, but first he must deal with George and the missing orders. With an effort, he pulled himself away from the pleasant scene, cleared his throat, and returned his attention to the still-smirking Duke.

"She has a way with clothing, does she not?" George drawled.

"Yes," Harry snipped, "though, they have been rather up and down of late."

George raised a bewildered brow, and Harry realized the Duke had not been present during Lady Avery's scene earlier that evening.

"It is of no consequence," Harry said, momentarily thrown off balance. His plan to gauge where George's loyalty lay through a carefully orchestrated conversation about the young Queen now seemed as transparent as his mother's cries for attention. "Perhaps we had best retire to the library for a glass of something," Harry suggested and led an inquisitive George out of the room. However, once they were ensconced on the sofa in the book-lined room, brandy snifters in hand, Harry still hadn't any idea of how to initiate a conversation that would lead to the recovery of his missing orders.

The Duke swirled the brandy around in his glass and waited, while Harry, suddenly aware of how potentially dangerous his situation was, reminded himself of the letter he was duty bound to deliver, the failure of which might mean the life of the Queen.

George gave Harry a dubious look and sipped some of his drink. "Very smooth," he said shortly, leaving Harry with the distinct impression the Duke did not refer to alcohol.

"I believe the best are meant to be," Harry countered.

His guest took another sip and rolled it about his mouth. "There's better out there."

"Doubtless true, but none other so close to hand," Harry replied with a careless shrug then cursed himself for having let slip the fact that he was entirely alone; unless, of course, it *were* brandy under discussion.

"One must contrive when the prize is so dear," George drawled.

It was Harry's turn to raise a brow. "I hadn't known you cared so much. Should I count you an admirer?"

"What else should I be?" the young Duke asked. "It would hardly do to upset the apple cart at this point."

His reply was non-committal at best, and Harry felt nowhere closer to the truth as to George's loyalties to the Queen as he had at the outset. But were they discussing the Queen or were they still on the subject of Harry as a secret service agent? He stood and went to the credenza to pour another drink, this time mostly water.

"It's not as if I don't know what you're up to," George claimed.

Harry froze, the decanter of water in his hand, and shifted to block George's view of the proceedings. "Whatever can you mean?"

"What else *can* I mean?" the Duke said with a snort. "You think yourself quite clever, I imagine."

Harry, still unsure of exactly what was under discussion, suddenly thought of a means of finding out; when at Eton, George had quite the reputation for having no tolerance for liquor whatsoever. Harry took up the brandy and splashed a double into George's snifter. "No, Your Grace, not clever. I'm simply a man with a mission."

"Exactly what might that mission be?" George demanded.

"The pursuit of the best brandy, what else?" Harry replied and downed the contents of his snifter. Suspicious, George did the same. Harry poured the Duke a robust refill, then turned his back, and filled his own snifter once again with water.

"You can't be serious!" George scoffed. "Get to the point and tell me what this is all about."

"It's about a lovely young woman," Harry said.

"That tells me nothing," George grumbled into his snifter. "There are more than a few of those about."

Harry drank deeply of his water and continued. "One whose impending nuptials have caused a bit of a stir."

"Your sham of a pretense makes me laugh," George said, but it seemed the brandy was not a matter for derision for he held out his snifter for another.

Harry smiled, delighted in more ways than one. "The question is, are you for or against it?"

"For or against what?" the Duke demanded in a voice that had started to slur.

"The marriage!" Harry retorted.

"It depen's on whom the bridegroom is, o'course," George mumbled.

Harry allowed the brandy decanter to hover over George's snifter. "German or French?"

George stared at the stream of brandy as it poured, glittering, into his snifter, his brow furrowed with concentration. "Neither!" he said emphatically.

Harry was taken aback. He was not aware there was a third option. Victoria could hardly marry a British prince, as there were none suitable to be had. A Russian prince would hardly be viewed as more favorable than a German one, and the prince of Sweden was already married, while the prince of Denmark had recently been through a scandalous divorce. No, he would never do.

Harry thought of the plan to assassinate the young Queen over her choice of bridegroom and decided to put the question to George that mattered most. "It's certainly not a killing matter for you, though, is it? Am I wrong to believe that you, as Duke of Marcross, are above that sort of thing?"

"I'd put a bullet in anyone who got in my way," George said with a slur of his words and a wave of his snifter that resulted in brandy sloshing up over the sides.

"Your Grace, I own I am a bit appalled," Harry insisted as he attempted to fill up the Duke's wildly bobbing snifter. "I've never seen you as a blood-thirsty man."

"You said it yoursel'. I have my position to think of. I'm the youngest duke in the land. Were you aware of tha', Haversham?" George asked and followed it up with a thorough draining of his snifter. "I shall be a peer of the realm for a long time to come and I shall have matters arranged to my satisfaction. Mine!" he said, hammering his chest with his free hand.

"But what of her wishes? Hasn't she the right to marry whom she chooses?" Harry demanded.

"No," George said as he wagged his head back and forth in exaggerated arcs. "Too young. She don't know by half what's suitable. Women need a firm hand to guide them," he managed to say just before he slid down the length of the leather sofa and dropped his snifter on the floor with a distinct tinkle of breaking glass.

Harry set down his own glass and began a thorough inspection of George's pockets; with any luck he had brought the paper with him rather than having left it unattended at home. Harry felt a surge of excitement when the crackle of vellum assailed his ears and a deep sense of relief when he had spread it open and verified that it was indeed his missing orders.

Harry was not as cheerful about his instructions, however. He was expected to keep the letter meant to accompany these orders under close guard as he retired to Dover to await further orders, most likely to board ship for parts unknown. How could he leave Mira now, with so much unsaid between them? Besides, he could hardly protect Mira from George if he left London. It would prove difficult to protect the Queen from George if he left Dover as well, but his orders were clear, and Harry was already nearly twenty-four hours behind in their execution.

He put the paper outlining his orders in the flames of the fireplace and removed all signs of the spree of drunken depravity he forced upon George, whom Harry settled more comfortably upon the sofa before he quit the room. His thoughts were dark and full of despair until he recalled Cedars, his country house along the Marine Parade in Dover, the one that came with the title, Viscount Haversham. It wasn't of his own comfort he thought; Cedars was large and sat on a cliff overlooking the ocean, the perfect setting for a house party. He would invite the Crenshaws, including the shifty Duke, and keep everyone as close as possible until his next orders arrived.

However, this plan presented a bit of a poser when it came to Harry's mother. He had no hope at all whatsoever that she would feel disinclined to attend such an event. What new horrors awaited his guests under the roof at Cedars with Lady Avery in attendance? And what of Mira? Would she ever agree to be his viscountess if he couldn't find his mother a more suitable means through which to acquire the constant attention she craved?

He caught a strain of music from the drawing room and remembered how hopeful he had felt about this ball, one which should have included making amends to Mira. Instead, he had danced with another girl and stood by and watched as Mira tended to his mother. How kind Mira had been! How erratic he must seem in her eyes! The retrieval of his orders was paramount, and the reason for his impromptu party in the first place, however, Harry couldn't help but feel that he had left his true work for last and went in search of the one who meant most to him in the world.

When he returned to the drawing room, he expected to find Mira, an excellent dancer, making the most of a contradanse. Instead, he spotted her seated in a corner across the room in conversation with his mother. He had always known Mira to be as beautiful as she was intelligent, however, at this moment the beauty of her benevolence outshone even the sapphire of her eyes. As he witnessed her tender ministrations to his mother, he was gripped with a sudden, intense, and all-encompassing sensation; he must make Mira Crenshaw his own. She was much more than he had ever supposed, and he wasn't worthy to so much as buckle her shoe; nevertheless, he vowed then and there that he would not rest until this kind-hearted, generous-spirited girl was plaited, inexorably, to his side.

So deep in conversation were Mira and his mother that they appeared startled when he presented himself and executed a deep bow. "Mother, should I be a boor if I were to claim Miss Crenshaw's hand for the next dance?" he asked with what he feared was a besotted grin, one impossible to suppress.

"Of course, Herbert," his mother replied, "but I do not like being deprived of her company for so long," she added with a moue.

"Then I trust you comprehend my current state of devastation," he replied. His look of intense longing was for Mira alone, who blushed and looked hastily away.

Lady Avery, whom Harry had rarely seen so happy and relaxed, rapped him on the arm with her fan and uttered a tsk. "You really should be less neglectful!" she insisted, but whether her admonition was for her own sake or Mira's, he could not guess.

"I cannot deny the truth of that," he said and drew up a chair to join them until the next dance, which, by his calculations, should be another waltz. "I find I am in need of a rest," he mused.

"And to think, you have danced but the once!" Mira quipped.

"If it please you, I intend to dance the rest of the evening," he said as clearly as he dared, for he knew not whether she would refuse all other partners and he would not dance at all if it could not be with her. "But it is not to dancing that I refer. My years of travel have made me long for a respite at the seashore."

Mira gave him an arch look. "I would not have thought rusticating in Italy and France so tedious a prospect."

Harry knew he deserved her censure but pressed on. "My months abroad were surprisingly eventful, though not in the way you might suppose," he hastened to add upon noting her frown. "I occupied myself greatly in the learning of languages, as well as the development of skills I had not the time to acquire as a schoolboy."

"Well, I should love a respite at the seashore above all things!" Lady Avery remarked with her usual enthusiasm. "Though I am persuaded it depends upon whom our hostess shall be."

"I thought to invite a great number of guests to Cedars and make it a regular house party; you might be my hostess, Mother, if you are up to it."

"Me? Your hostess?" she asked with a flurry of tiny claps. "In that, case, I know I shall have a lovely time! I am such an excellent hostess," she remarked in an aside to Mira, "and am sure to treat myself with the deference owed my station."

Harry noted the flash of surprise that crossed Mira's face and hastened to explain. "Cedars is my country house in Dover. Mother would doubtless enjoy more rest were she to remain in London, nevertheless, I was persuaded once she learned of my plans she would insist on being in attendance. Now, Mother, I promise not to expect of you more than you are able. Perhaps Miss Crenshaw shall take pity on you and be an arm to lean on in a pinch," he proposed, fully aware of the risk he took.

"I should be delighted to assist Lady Avery in any way possible," Mira replied but Harry detected the hesitance in her voice. It was then that the contradanse came to an end, and the babble that always arose on such an occasion filled the air.

"We shall discuss it further while we dance," Harry said. He stood and offered his hand to Mira who took it and rose to her feet.

"I shall return presently," Mira promised Lady Avery with a smile before she gave Harry leave to lead her to the center of the room where they waited for the music to begin, their glances coming together to cling for a moment before they skittered away.

Harry was painfully aware of Mira's agitation and prayed he hadn't overstepped his bounds. He waited until the music started so as to speak to her in relative privacy, but as they began to move to the music, he found himself caught up in the sensation of her hand in his own, so small and delicate, the other feather-light on his shoulder. The feel of his hand clasped round her tiny waist made him feel large and oafish in comparison, and he was afraid he would tread on her toes with his suddenly enormous feet. He reminded himself that he had danced all over Europe, indeed, had waltzed with a young lady only an hour since, and she had nothing of which to complain. With a mental shake, he took himself in hand and offered his apologies.

"I pray I have not distressed you with my talk of a house party," he started. "I realize it was a great assumption on my part to include you in my plans but I see how good you are with my mother and I must admit, I am rather desperate."

"Desperate? To throw a party?" Mira asked, clearly puzzled.

"No," Harry said with a chuckle. "You are correct, a house party is not a desperate matter. However, I am wishful of removing from London to Dover for a time. It would be a pity to deprive myself of society in the middle of the Season, so why not bring society along?"

"And your mother? Do not say that after four years abroad you cannot bear to be parted from her now," Mira said with a pointed look.

"Then I shall not," he replied, matching her look with his own. "In truth, after four years abroad, a man does not return home on account of his mother." He thought he saw a light flare in her eyes and took heart. "It is perhaps presumptuous of me to assume you on hand for such an event. This is your debutante Season after all, and there is the Duke of Marcross to consider." He drew a deep breath and searched her eyes for what seemed an eternity, but she did not reply. When a surge of pain assailed his lungs, he realized he had ceased to breathe and released the stale air in a long sigh. "Say you will come, Mira," he begged with a squeeze to her hand. He would not, could not, leave her. Not again. Nevertheless, he filled his memory with every detail of her face in the case they were parted after all.

Mira seemed not to notice his scrutiny. It was as if she were in a world of her own, and he was a bit taken aback when she spoke.

"Are you quite sure you must go?" she asked very matter-of-factly, as if she understood much more than he had supposed.

He felt relief wash through his veins. "Your gift for perception fills me with admiration. Indeed, I have no choice in the matter," he admitted. "I have so longed for the association of your brothers and esteemed parents. Do you think they would follow you to Dover should I invite them?"

"You are obliged to ask! You must see that I can hardly make a journey to Dover on my own. And George will not hear of it if he is not to be one of the party as well."

Harry nodded and allowed his thoughts to be swallowed up in the music for a turn or two about the room before he returned to the subject of George. The concern he felt at the thought of Mira's marriage to the Duke amounted almost to panic; he would not have her endure the trials of marriage to a traitor. If he were honest, that was as selfless as he was likely to become on the matter. The thought of being parted from her produced a pain so fierce it brought him out in a sweat and made him weak in the knees. He hadn't any notion of how much time in England remained to him but he must make every moment count.

"Mira," he prompted and waited until she turned to face him and he could meet her eyes with his own. "Do you wish to marry the Duke?"

"I only wish to make my parents happy," she said with such clarity and swiftness that Harry could not doubt it to be her primary motivation.

"Does *your* happiness mean nothing to them?"

"Yes, of course it does! Only, they feel they are more suitable judges as to what shall constitute such happiness than am I."

"And they believe your cousin will make you happier than . . . than another?" Harry asked, hesitant to reveal the state of his heart before he was more familiar with hers.

"Perhaps, though they have not always." She looked away, unwilling to meet his gaze.

"I had not thought them to be so changeable," Harry accused.

"Nor they you," she shot back then, with a deep sigh, appeared to relent. "Oh, Harry! I know it is not your wish to hurt me and I will always stand your friend . . . no matter what else might happen," she added, her voice choking a little. "For I will not go against my parents."

Harry verged on asking if she did not love him more than that but swallowed the words. It was a question to which she very well might not yet know the answer. "Have I lost all hope, then, of their regard?" he asked instead.

"I don't know," she said with a shake of her head. She paused and gave him a keen look from eyes so blue, he found it difficult to think of aught else. "Keep your secrets if you must, Harry. I shall stand by you until you are free to tell me all. However, until my parents understand why you stayed away so long with no word and why you behaved such a fribble upon your return, they will not look on you with favor. And now you must dash off when the Season has barely begun! What are they to think?"

"You are quite right," he said with a slow nod. "I can see that my actions have sunk me below reproach. But, why George?" he demanded, barely able to conceal his frustration. "It is clear to me you are unable to tolerate the man. Have you reflected on how marriage to him will rob you of your happiness? Are they so bent on garnering you the highest title possible?"

"Harry! You know my parents care little for such things! Perhaps you are not aware of how they once despised each other. As such, I believe they do not necessarily see our mutual dislike as an impediment to the development of an attachment at some point in the future."

These were surprising words indeed, however, Harry refused to give up. "Your father and mother are renowned for their obvious affection for one another, this is true, and you must know that I hold your parents in higher esteem than my own parents or any others'," Harry said with a wealth of frustration that resulted in a jerk of his hand at her waist. It brought Mira a shade closer in proximity than the steps of the dance warranted, but he was past caring what others thought—save her parents. "But their case is not yours. You say they despised each other, yes? And you might very well despise the Duke. But what George feels for you isn't anything as warm as that. He neither despises you nor loves you; you are merely a means to an end, someone on whom he wastes little thought except how, in spite of no official declaration, you belong to him—exactly as does his race horse. There is no hope that his utter lack of feeling could one day turn to love of any kind."

He would have gone on but he noted how her face had drained of color and thought better of it. He was at a loss as to what could have caused such distress until he felt a tap on his shoulder and turned to see the Duke of Marcross, his face dark as thunder.

"I must insist you allow me the remainder of this dance!"

"Your Grace, you are drunk," Harry said and turned away, but George would have none of it.

"Perhaps," he said exactly as if he weren't speaking into the back of Harry's head. "But I can still stand and I'll be damned if you dance one more step with my intended bride."

Harry whirled to once again face the Duke and put out an arm to prevent Mira from participating in their exchange. "Then to hell you must go. Who are you to decide with whom Miss Crenshaw dances? The papers have been decidedly bereft of any mention of her betrothal to you or any other."

"Harry," Mira hissed in his ear. "There must not be another scene tonight, not on my account. I could not bear it." He paid her words no heed, however, until he felt the touch of her gloved hand against his palm as she entwined her fingers in his. "Invite us, and I will see to it that we come," she whispered, then let go, and made her way to the side of her cousin. "George, it is good of you to join us. I thought perhaps you had already departed." And with that she put her hand in his and waltzed away.

Harry could not abide the thought of standing by whilst Mira danced all night with the Duke of Marcross. However, he could hardly quit his own event. As such, he must remain and see to the comfort of his guests. But he did not dance.

chapter eleven

Mira waltzed with George even as her thoughts were with Harry. She watched as he went to speak with his mother, who pouted and stamped her foot in response to whatever it was he had to say. It was distressing to see how much persuasion was required in order for Harry to help her regain control of her temper.

"Surely, you cannot be so obsessed with him," George sneered.

Mira turned her attention to her cousin with a start. "I can't think what you mean," she said with a careless shrug.

"It's not what *I* mean," George drawled. "It's what *he* means to do," he said with a jerk of his chin in Harry's direction.

Mira turned to look and observed Harry, now by the fireplace in conversation with a group of gentlemen.

"Why? Is he up to something untoward?" she replied, though her attention remained with Harry long enough to see him turn away from his guests to meet her gaze as the waltz brought her nearly close enough for the hem of her gown to sweep across his feet.

"He means to thwart me at every turn," George huffed and aimed a glare straight down his pointed nose at Mira.

"You needn't look as if you intend to eat me! And if you refer to Lord Haversham, I fear I remain at an utter loss."

George had the grace to look discomfited. "It is not fitting that I should condemn a man before he has made his actions known to the world."

"If by that statement you refer to his intention to woo me out from under you," Mira said with a smile of pure sweetness, "I suppose you may be correct."

George pressed his lips together and said nothing. Grateful for the respite, Mira found her attention once again wander to Harry. She thought it odd that there were female guests who were without a partner, including Lucy Sutherland, and yet Harry did not dance. Once again, as she sailed past him, his green and steady gaze lifted from his study of the carpet to look into her eyes.

"I wonder that your father has allowed you any association with Haversham at all whatsoever," George said in low tones. "Lord Avery is a buffoon, Lady Avery displays her lack of breeding at every opportunity, and the Viscount, himself, is nothing but a charlatan."

"Why?" Mira asked, alarmed. "Do you consider his odd behavior as of late to be a pretense?"

"Odd indeed!" George insisted. "He swings back and forth between acting the fool and behaving as if he is superior to everyone he encounters."

"Surely, you can't mean to say he believes *you* his inferior," Mira said with an arch smile.

Her contempt was lost on George, however. "But, of course! He makes his position clear when he apes his betters as he does tonight. He can't have learned such passable tastes in manner and dress from his family."

Mira knew the equity of that statement and bit back a smile. "He did spend four years on the Continent.

Surely that might account for any degree of evolution in a man."

"Ah! Then how does one account for his behavior as of late?" George asked just as Mira spotted the weakness in her argument.

"Whatever the reason for his earlier behavior, he has since gained perspective," she said with a lift of her chin. "I should be astounded were he to abandon his current mode of dress and graceful demeanor," Mira predicted. Had she not made it clear that her mama and papa would never allow their daughter to marry such a dolt as Bertie? "In fact, I drew Bertie's attention to the matter only tonight," she said with a bright smile.

"Is that so?" George asked. "And what was *Bertie's* response? I am all agog."

"He expressed an implacable desire to mend his ways, that is all," Mira said, uncomfortably aware that he had done nothing of the sort as she gazed once again over George's shoulder to where Harry stood bent over the ear trumpet of an elderly woman who sat alone in a corner of the room. He gave every impression of being fully engaged in their conversation; Mira thought surely he would not notice her passing. However, at the last moment, he spotted her from the corner of his eye, straightened out to his full height and met her gaze with a frank one of his own that sent the butterflies in Mira's stomach into full flutter.

"I am surprised to hear you own he is in want of a lesson or two," George quipped. "You have been so blindly enamored of him since you were a child, in spite of everything."

"You speak in riddles, Your Grace."

"Do not be so obtuse, Mira, it does not become you. Admit it, you have long made a habit of trailing after him."

"If by that you refer to my desire to be with my brothers, one can hardly find me guilty of anything more. The fact that Har—ah, Bertie wished to be near them as well is neither here nor there."

"Do you deny, then, your affection for him?"

Mira risked a glance over George's shoulder in time to lock gazes with Harry once more. It felt as if he were privy to their conversation, and she smiled at the bubble of happiness that rose within her.

"The very least you owe me is the truth. If you think I do not see how you simper at him even now, you must think me the sorriest of fools. Your shameless flirting dishonors me, and I will not countenance it," George insisted. "I wonder that your parents can have done so little to suppress your infatuation of him. Were you my daughter, I would have done so, certainly when news of the boating accident came to my ears, if not before."

"How does the boating accident signify in the least?" Mira asked, surprised that George should bring it up but grateful for the chance to put him to the question.

"If your parents had favored you with the truth, you would have no need to question me on the subject!"

"I am quite aware of the boating accident; have no fears on that score!" Mira said in defense of her parents whilst heartily disappointed that it disallowed her from further questioning as she dared not expose her ignorance on the matter.

"Then you are fully aware of how unsuitable he is for all but the most desperate of spinsters."

Mira was forced into silence by that statement. She couldn't fathom why the accident should bring so much shame to Harry. She hadn't known, either, that the exchanged glances between herself and Harry were so apparent. The thought made her burn with chagrin, and she forced herself not to so much as glance past George's shoulder for the remainder of the set.

When the music came to a close, George refused to turn her loose until he had located Mira's parents and delivered her safely into their keeping. They were discovered on the ground floor in the otherwise deserted dining room as they sat together on a small sofa by the fire. Sir Anthony had his arm about his lady as he fed her apple slices from his fingers, and she, in turn, glowed at his tenderness. Neither seemed to notice that they were no longer alone and looked up in surprise when George made his presence known with a deep cough.

Mira thought her father looked a bit abashed, but her mother merely laughed and jumped to her feet to fix them plates of their own. Mira could not help but notice how her father's gaze was fastened on his wife as she went round the table collecting bits and pieces from each platter and wondered that she did not feel flustered as she most often did by her father's obvious affection for her mother. Instead, Mira felt an envy that pierced her soul. If this was what it was like to love and be loved, then there was no hope for her and George. When her mother approached her with a plate of fruit and sandwiches, Mira refused it and abandoned George to sit by her father on the sofa.

"Papa," she whispered. "I find I have the headache and must go home."

"I would not be in the least surprised if your mother shouldn't wish to go home as well," her father said, placing an arm around her shoulders and giving her a gentle squeeze. "Let us leave your brothers to fend for themselves and bespeak our carriage."

"Thank you, Papa!" Mira replied as she leaned into the circle of his arm. "I am afraid George will be angry with me but I find I do not mind so much if he is."

Sir Anthony frowned. "What right has George to be angry with you?"

"He hasn't," Mira said once she had ensured George was too caught up in conversation with her mama to eavesdrop. "Nevertheless, he is continually finding fault with me. When he last dined with us, he was dreadfully rude and even grasped my arm quite painfully."

Her father's frown deepened, and Mira felt how his tension rose as he prepared to speak. Fearing the worst, she put a hand to his knee and said, "No, Papa. I do not wish there to be a scene. Poor Bertie has had more to deal with than any man should tonight already."

"It is good of you to consider his feelings," her father replied, his frown all but vanished. "Am I wrong to suppose your previous feelings of affection for him have not undergone a serious alteration?"

"No, Papa, not wrong, but your wishes do and must remain my primary desire."

"Then rest assured that my wishes are for you to be as content in your marriage as are your mother and I," he said with a pat to her hand. "In point of fact, we have long believed Harry, that is to say, Bertie, to be the man for you."

Mira felt her heart leap in her chest. "Truly, Papa? For Mama does not seem to think so and says I am not old enough to be wise in such matters."

"Perhaps she is right. Whatever his name, he has not been himself as of late," her father mused. "However, I find I cannot like George, no matter how convinced I am that I would be a fool to rob you of such a brilliant marriage."

"Brilliant? How can you say so, Papa?" Mira objected. "Rather, I would say commiserable, infelicitous, and fallacious."

"Ah, Mira, so fond of your dictionary," her father said, tightening the circle of his arm around her shoulders. "However, let us not get too far ahead of ourselves," he warned. "You have registered your complaints, and now it is for me to air my concerns. If Bertie had behaved ever since his return as he has tonight, I would have done all in my power to further your attachment to him. However, as things stand, he appears to be a bit unsteady. One would not go too far to call his mother more than a little deranged, and I fear for his offspring if not for Har . . . Bertie himself."

Mira yearned to speak in Harry's defense, but George had stepped away from her mother and looked as if he intended to join the conversation with her father. "Please, Papa, I don't wish to speak of it in front of George," she whispered, and then he was upon them.

"This is quite the *tete-a-tete* you are having," he said, but Sir Anthony rose to his feet and held out his hand to Mira before George could complete his sentence.

"I'm afraid my daughter feels ill and wishes to depart."

Mira and her mother shared a glance. "I don't believe I have ever seen you look so pale, my darling," Lady Crenshaw said and hurried to Mira's side to put a hand to her forehead. "I think it would be wise to do as your father says. George, would you be so good as to request that Adrian or Stephen have our carriage brought round?" she asked.

George, his distaste for her choice of address plain on his face, seemed to struggle with his thoughts until he finally executed a short bow and quit the room.

Once the door had shut firmly behind him, Lady Crenshaw turned to her daughter in alarm. "Mira, what is it? I have not seen you so distressed since your canary died when you were four years old."

"Mama, you cannot possibly believe that to have been the height of my despair!" Mira cried and rushed to put her arms around her mother to weep against her neck. "I was far more distressed when Harry did not return after Eton, if you recall."

"Is he whom this is about?" her mother asked.

"No, it's about George. He is odious beyond words! And that scene with Lady Avery—how Harry, that is, Bertie must have wished to expire on the spot! And then George would not allow me to dance with Harry, and I was so angry at him but I did not wish to cause Harry any more distress and so I danced with George after all, and he was odious!"

"Yes, I do believe you have mentioned that more than once. However, I think perhaps this is not so much about the 'odious' George," her mother said gently, "but how much you care for Harry."

"Bertie," Mira said with a sniff, pulling away from her mother and taking the handkerchief she offered. She wiped her eyes and blew her nose as she carefully considered what it was she should say next. "He wishes to be called

Bertie; I don't know why, but I feel it is important to honor his request. Meanwhile, I merely wish to convey to you how much I despise George and how unfair everyone has been to Bertie, that is all."

"Yes, we are quite familiar with how much you despise George," her mother urged.

"Well, I am not," her father said as he put an arm around Lady Crenshaw's waist. "Let us hear her out."

"Thank you, Papa! I only ask that you give Bertie a chance. He is not deranged, as much as you fear he may be, and Mama, you may have once despised Papa, but it is not the same with George. It cannot be!"

Her father regarded her mother in surprise. "You despised me?" he asked in mock dismay.

"I never said so!" Lady Crenshaw insisted. "I would say, rather, 'disliked.' However, there is no doubt I was the last young lady you should have chosen for your wife if it weren't for Grandaunt Regina's interference."

"I owe her an undying debt of gratitude, to be sure." Sir Anthony averred. "However, I like to think that I should have eventually come to my senses on my own. In the interim, I never thought you odious, not for one moment."

"Nor I you," his wife admitted, blushing.

"So, you see, I do believe what Mira feels for George is not the same degree of dislike we experienced at the outset of our association," her father explained.

"I admit, I am *most* relieved," Lady Crenshaw said. "I have never thought George right for you, Mira, but feared that if I said as much, you would immediately develop an attachment to him out of pure pique. Then where should we be?"

"Then you don't wish me to marry George?" Mira asked, too confounded to take umbrage at her mother's connivance.

"Not I!" her mother insisted. "However, I felt it best for you to learn where your own heart leads."

"And Papa?" Mira asked, still feeling too bewildered to comprehend exactly where it was her parents stood on the matter.

"I, as does your mother, feel we are wiser than your youth will allow. Nevertheless, you have always put me far too much in mind of your great-grandmother to press you. Nor would I wish to," her father said with a fond smile.

Hope surged in Mira's breast. I own that Bertie has seemed more than a little odd since his return, but if he continues to behave more becomingly, Mama, and were he to ask Papa for permission to court me, would you object?"

"Not on his own account alone" her mother replied. "However, there is still his mother to consider. I wonder if anyone's reputation could withstand such nonsense on a regular basis. It is sad but true that society will tar you with the same brush. You might find that you are making for yourself an intolerable circumstance in which to abide."

Mira pressed her hands together in supplication. "Tonight, when Lady Avery carried on so shockingly, I could not help but note the look on Bertie's face; I thought my heart would break. What he must have felt! Yet, I am persuaded it would not be fair to him if I did not afford him time to take his mother in hand. I do believe he might, if only his father does not interfere."

Mira carefully observed her parents as they looked at each other and back at her with eyes full of compassion.

"There is no doubt that your affection for Lord Haversham is strong," her mother said. "As to whether or not it is a friendship that can grow into something more, in spite of his mother . . ."

"Let us not forget his father," Sir Anthony interjected.

"Yes, in spite of his mother and his father both, remains to be seen," Lady Crenshaw explained.

"Bertie is far more than a friend," Mira retorted but refrained from further elucidation on that score when she realized that an argument would most likely as not undo all she had accomplished. "Perhaps you are correct and what I feel for him is naught but friendship; I have never before been in love. But will you afford us the opportunity to sort it out for ourselves?"

"Yes," her father said. "But he must prove to us that he will make you a most satisfactory husband and a devoted father to our grandchildren."

"And that he will take his mother in hand and put an end to further scenes such as we witnessed tonight," her mother added with deep sigh.

"Oh, thank you!" Mira cried. She felt the need to clap her hands with joy but suppressed the urge in the nick of time. She knew that were she to develop that habit, all hopes of marriage to Harry would be at an end.

It was then that the door opened, and a clutch of guests entered the room to descend on the platters of wilted sandwiches and browned apple slices. Behind them followed Adrian. "Your carriage awaits your pleasure," he said with a bow for his parents and an arm for Mira.

"Do you go home as well, Adrian?" Mira asked as they trailed after their parents.

"I think not," Adrian replied. "I do, however, think Lucy Sutherland grows prettier with every passing moment."

"Lord Haversham might take exception to your claim on her," Mira bantered as she caught, from the corner of her eye, the subject of her barb waiting by the front door. Somehow he looked more handsome than he had when she arrived, and her heart skipped a beat or two when he favored her with an uncertain smile. She wondered if she could ever tire of the lean planes of his face, the green of his almond-shaped eyes, or the way his blond hair curled along his forehead and ears.

She noted, also, that his jaw was tense, his hands were curled in knots at his sides, and he seemed unusually alert, a circumstance she supposed was due to the presence of George, who stood between Harry and the door as if the Duke were the evening's host. She counted the seconds until it was her turn to say goodbye, but George indicated a stern resolve to remain, making any private exchange of words with Harry quite impossible. She felt the disappointment rise into her throat and draw it tight.

Hoping Harry would read her thoughts on her face, Mira extended her hand to him, but George stepped forward and seized it with the speed of a viper. She gasped, but Harry maintained an admirable composure quite at odds with Adrian's, whose arm tensed under her own. Quickly, she turned to flash him a look of warning and wondered how to forestall the inevitable flying of fists but was saved the trouble when her brother dropped her arm and stormed out the door. Save the butler, she was now left alone with George and Harry, a circumstance for which she felt no undue amount of misgiving.

"I would thank you, George, to let go of my hand," she said in a cool voice designed to communicate her disdain. He, however, seemed unaffected by her disapproval and kissed her gloved hand before he presented it to Harry with a great show of proprietorship.

Something dangerous and wholly unfamiliar moved in Harry's eyes, and, of a sudden, Mira wished Adrian had remained at her side. George, seemingly unaware of his danger, was little threat to Harry but she feared the pathetically thin Duke would be killed by one blow should there be no one to forestall Harry. She looked to the butler whose stare remained trained on the wall across from him as if supremely unaware of anything untoward having occurred. Just when she felt the matter must come to blows after all, Harry turned on his heel and walked away so abruptly that the pain squeezed the air from her lungs.

A look of scorn crossed George's face. "His mama doubtless has need of him," he said, just before Harry returned with a pair of very tall footmen in his wake. Each took hold of one of the Duke's arms and stalked off with him up the stairs as he struggled and sputtered his noncompliance. The butler followed the trio up the stairs, and Mira watched their departure with keen pleasure as George's cries grew fainter and fainter and she and Harry were at last alone, or would have been if Adrian hadn't chosen that moment to return inside.

"Mira, they are waiting on you!"

Crestfallen, she turned to follow her brother out the door, but Harry took her hand and pulled her back to his side.

"Adrian," he said in a voice that brooked no argument, "Miss Crenshaw will be out presently. Do shut the door behind you as you leave," he said, his gaze fixed fast to Mira's face all the while. When the sound of Adrian's departing footsteps ceased, Harry took a deep breath and let it out as if finally rid of a great burden.

Just when she thought there must be something terribly wrong with her face that he should stare at it so, he smiled just as he had in days of old and she felt, for the first time, that Harry was finally home. He looked down at her hand in his and brought it up for the kiss for which she had had pined all evening. However, she was more than a little surprised when he turned it over and drew the top of her fashionably short glove down with the tip of his finger to expose her wrist, and, bringing it to his lips, kissed it, slowly and gently, as if this act were the sole fruition of his dreams.

Despite the increased flow of blood to her brain, Mira could think of no words for what she felt. Even if she had, her heart beat so fast, she could not draw breath to speak. Clearing her throat, she found herself enough recovered to squeak out a thin "goodnight."

"Until Dover," he said, and, with a great show of reluctance, released her hand. She knew she must depart, but neither of them moved. The air between them seemed a palpable obstacle too great to conquer, yet he managed to reach across it to take hold of a red-gold curl and caress it between his trembling fingers.

Mira was once again left to wonder what could be so intriguing about her hair that could be so worthy of his notice even while her body seemed to comprehend what her mind could not fathom. The knowledge filled her with a sensation of warmth that spread from her center to flood her entire being.

Suddenly, his gaze flew again to her face, his cheeks ruddy with chagrin as if caught out in the middle of some imprudent act. He opened his mouth and took a breath as if he were about to speak, then seemed to change his mind, and dropped the curl with an air of defeat.

"Harry, what is it?" she asked and the air between them shifted as if he had taken a step towards her though she knew he had not stirred.

He pinned her gaze in his own and swallowed hard, lifted his hands as if to take her by the shoulders, then dropped them again to hang in fists at his sides. The air between them pressed against her as if in demand of she knew not what, and he moved towards her to fill the space that divided them. When she did not move or flee or faint, he took a step closer until nothing separated them but her hands against his chest so that she could feel how fast his heart beat beneath her palms.

"Do not," he said in a voice as breathless as she felt, "marry George."

"I won't," Mira promised.

"Even should your parents wish it?" he demanded as he searched her eyes.

"I . . . I don't think they shall."

He closed his eyes and swallowed hard. "And if they do?" When she didn't answer, his eyes flew open, and she read his heart in them.

"Oh, Harry," she said and reached up to put her hand against his cheek and marveled at how scratchy and unyielding and utterly foreign-smelling yet utterly familiar all at the same time. "I have spoken with them, and they have agreed to give you a chance."

He swallowed again and put up a hand to cover hers, his breathing more labored with every moment. With a small cry of relief, he dropped his forehead to rest against hers and slid his free hand up her back to rest at the base of her neck. Without knowing why, she closed her eyes and focused on the sound of his breathing, extraordinarily aware of the proximity of his mouth to hers.

"No matter what happens," he said, his voice rough, "I beg you to know that I love you. I always have, and always shall. You must promise that you will never doubt it."

Mira wished to nod her head to indicate her assent but knew it to be too dangerous as it would put her lips in a compromising position. Nevertheless, when his fingers slid up to tangle in her hair, the breath caught in her throat and her chin lifted of its own accord. With a little tug, he pulled her mouth to his and her senses reeled at the merest touch of his lips to her own.

He moved over her mouth as he had her wrist, slowly and gently with a sweetness that brought tears to her eyes, his lips taking hers from one corner to the next, savoring everything in between, as if it were the last kiss they would ever share. She felt a moan rise in her throat, and her lips parted as if in obedience to a command she could not have known to give. With another groan, his arms came around her as he pulled her closer than she thought possible, and he deepened the kiss until she became dizzy and limp and her knees buckled beneath her.

Immediately, he pulled away, and she opened her eyes in surprise to find him looking at her in alarm.

"What is wrong?" she asked, alarmed on her own account.

"I thought perhaps you had fainted," he said in a voice so thick and husky that it sent a heretofore unknown shiver up her spine.

"Oh," she said, still more than a little breathless. "Should I have?"

He smiled in a way she had never before known him to smile, and she realized she was held in the arms of the new and fearless, possibly dangerous, Harry she had imagined and yearned for. She wished to speak to him, to put any number of questions to him, but her heart beat so fast she struggled to catch her breath. If only she could stay in his arms forever, but he loosened his hold on her, and there was naught she could do but test the dependability of her knees and attempt to stand on her own. Instead, she sagged against him so that he was forced to once again enfold her in his arms before she collapsed. He seemed to have no objection for he kissed her again, this time hard and searing hot as if branding her with his lips would make her his. Finally, with a deep sigh, he took her by the elbows and stepped back.

This time she managed to remain aloft and required only a moment before her head stopped spinning. She knew she had put off her departure far past what her parents would approve and moved towards the door. Harry seemed ready to allow her to leave for her went to the door as well and pulled it open.

"You will come to Dover?" he asked as if her response to his kiss hadn't promised him any manner of possibilities. She found herself nodding regardless, and took the arm he offered for her journey down the front steps to Adrian, who waited, impatiently, for Harry to relinquish Mira into his care.

Without a word, Adrian opened the carriage door, handed her in, put up the steps, and closed the door between herself and the person she loved more than any other.

chapter twelve

Harry watched the Crenshaw's carriage disappear into the night and told himself matters were not as dark as he feared, that he would see Mira again, that her parents would accept his invitation to come to Cedars, and that the orders he would find waiting for him there would not send him pelting into the night immediately upon his arrival.

He turned to Adrian who remained at his side and attempted a jovial smile. "I fear that I grow weary of London," he said shortly.

"The season has barely begun," Adrian replied with some surprise. "It's Mira's debutante Season; you can't mean to desert her!"

"Not at all. Rather, I hope for her to join me." Harry knew he was taking a risk by abandoning Bertie's asinine behavior for the moment, but he rather suspected Adrian would sprint away if Harry uttered even one obnoxious bark of laughter. Besides, Adrian was trustworthy, and Harry needed his old friend's help in achieving his goal. "I am to have a house party in Dover. Might I prevail upon your mother and father to allow her to attend? That is to say, your entire family are to be invited."

Adrian said nothing, but Harry saw the doubt cloud his eye in spite of the dying flames of the flambeaux on every side.

"I fully comprehend your reservations," Harry urged in a low voice, "but matters are not as they seem."

"Do you mean to say that you did not appear at my house less than a week past dressed like a jackanapes and calling yourself Bertie? Heaven knows you will not win fair maiden behaving as such," he said with a jerk of his head in the direction of the departed carriage.

"I am persuaded Miss Crenshaw's affections are fixed, regardless of what I wear or how I am addressed," Harry said stiffly.

"It is not Mira's feelings under discussion. If you find her essential to your happiness, you must convince harder hearts than that of my sister."

"And what of the state of your heart, Adrian? Is it as hard as all that?"

"There was a time when I could not have wished for her a better man," Adrian replied with a shake of his head.

"And now?" Harry urged.

"I doubt I've seen her happier than just now. Who am I to stand in her way? However, I cannot endorse your cause with my father if you utter so much as a phrase *a la Francaise*," Adrian warned.

"And if I do?"

Adrian frowned. "You mustn't."

"But," Harry prodded, "you will see to it that your parents accept the invitation to the house party on behalf of your family?"

Adrian threw back his head and laughed. "You did not used to be quite so intractable. You must own that persuading them to leave London when Mira has just made her bows to be a very tall order."

"Of course, but I intend to invite the cream of society so her absence will be of no consequence."

"You believe that society will follow you into the country with the Season so fresh?" Adrian demanded.

"I do! They shall be eager to see what scrape my mother falls into next, shall they not?" Just as eager as was Harry to prove to Mira that his mother's next debacle would be her last.

"You are doubtless correct, but do you think your credit can stand it or are you already in one scandal too deep?"

"We shall find out, my friend," Harry said with a hand to Adrian's shoulder.

"Not so fast! I find I cannot endorse this plan unless certain persons are invited."

"Oh, and whom should I add to the list?" Harry asked, his interest piqued.

"To be fair, it's only one person. Rather, one person and her mother and father," Adrian amended.

"Ah!" Harry said, as light dawned. "Do I see wedding bells in Miss Sutherland's future?"

"Only if she says yes," Adrian replied with a broad smile.

"To that end I recommend a thorough kissing," Harry insisted as he turned to lead his guest up the steps into the house.

Light dawned for Adrian as well, and his smile dissolved into a scowl. "I think perhaps I should call you out for that!"

"Perhaps you should!" Harry laughed and opened the door to allow Adrian to enter. "However, I am persuaded you would much rather go in search of another dance with the lovely Lucy."

Adrian smiled broader than before. "You are a dashed sight too clever, Haversham," he said with a shake of his head, whereupon he went through the door and up the stairs, two at a time, to the room containing Miss Sutherland.

Harry, however, retired to the library where he sat by the fire and contemplated the evening's events. He had discovered that his mother was perfectly amendable to airing her shortcomings for the world to see, something he had formally believed to be a mostly private horror. He learned nothing definite from George, other than that he was a hopeless muttonhead, but was successful in the recovery of his orders in spite of it, or rather, because of it. Against all odds, a house party had been proposed and was going forth, and he had kissed Mira in a way so insistent, selfish, foolhardy, and irrevocable that she had little choice but to acquiesce.

The fact that she had so recently seemed resigned to marrying George proved how little she knew her own heart. Worse, in spite of his declaration of love, Harry was acutely aware that she had not professed her love in return. He knew he needed to take himself more in hand; he must go slowly and allow Mira to make her own choice. To that end, he would invite a number of gentlemen in want of a wife to the house party. It would necessitate invitations go to a number of eligible young ladies as well, and Harry trusted it would not raise hopes of an offer of marriage in the hearts of said young ladies nor their mothers. However, it would not do to have an uneven party.

He went to the desk, found paper and pen, and began his second guest list during the course of that day: Lucy Sutherland and her parents for Adrian, while Mira's bosom beau Viola Carlson-Johnson and her mama and papa would do for Stephen. The orphaned and single Mr. DiPastena and his sister, Jenny, would be balanced out by the unmarried Sir Hollis and his sister Heather, conveniently possessed of an elderly father who never ventured anywhere so no need to find him a partner at table. Giles Russell was led around by the nose by his widowed mother, and the widowed Marquess of Grandison led around by the nose by his unwed daughter, Ramona. Harry positively smelled a match or two somewhere amongst the four of them.

As he continued on with his list, he noticed that none of the gentlemen invited were likely in the least to suit Mira, but he pushed the thought aside; she must have the opportunity to spend time with other candidates for her hand. Those who were willing would each have his chance. He knew he must invite George in order to keep him under scrutiny and, therefore, his mother, also. As it turned out, they made a full twenty four, including himself, his mother, and his father, whom he hoped could be prevailed upon to attend.

It grew late, and his guests departing but Harry stayed at his desk and scratched out the needed invitations. He would leave for Dover at first light, immediately after he had seen to it that the invitations were hand delivered to his guests and a special messenger acquired to take a letter to his housekeeper and butler in Dover; it would never do to show up at Cedars unannounced.

He dated the party for two days hence which should give Harry time to hire the necessary help, have the furniture removed of its Holland covers, cleaned, polished, and bees-waxed into readiness. It would also give his guests the required time to make their arrangements and arrive, at the very latest, day after next in accordance with a late dinner or, perhaps, an early supper. He would plan menus for both as he was almost certainly more qualified to do so than his mother.

He was certain, also, that his mother was incapable of selecting her wardrobe in so short a time which would serve to delay her departure by at least several days. This bought him time with the Crenshaws prior to his mother's arrival even while it posed a different problem. As such, he hoped Lady Crenshaw would agree to be his hostess until Lady Avery's arrival and scratched a note on the Crenshaw invitation requesting her services. Why he was in such haste to retire from London and commence a house party without his mother immediately available to act as his hostess was a question society would beg be answered, but he would cross that bridge when he came to it. He counted on most being too polite to ask.

Finally, he was finished. With a yawn, he pulled the bell rope for the butler to take the invitations in hand and see to it that the fire was damped and the room tidied. He then wandered out to the front hall to bid goodnight to the last of his guests, whereupon he took the stairs up to the first floor, expecting to find the drawing room empty. Instead, he found his mother seated on the floor by her plinth, her arms stretched across it, her head to one side, fast asleep.

As he gazed down at her, he recognized that she very well might represent his largest challenge in the quest for Mira's hand in marriage. There were others: 'Bertie' would almost surely be needed to make an appearance which would upset the Crenshaws, Harry might find it necessary to quit his own house party at any time, his orders might involve any number of perilous instructions, and George, as well as any of the other gentlemen Harry invited, might eventually appeal to Mira in a way he did not. However, in spite of his personal doubts and fears, he sensed that the strength of their mutual attachment would rise above any and all of these matters but that of his troublesome, unpredictable, and foolish mother.

With a sigh, he lifted her into his arms and carried her up to the second floor to the bedrooms. He passed his father's room, his snores verification that he was only too happy to abdicate his responsibility for his wife to whomever was at hand. Once Harry had obtained his mother's room, a footman hurried forward to open the door, and Harry placed her on the bed and rang for her maid.

As he once again regarded his mother, still pretty after years of marriage to her affable but neglectful husband, Harry realized that she had stood in the way of his every success in life. It was she who had coddled him, fussed over him, denied him, over-protected him, and held him to such an unrealistic standard that he felt it useless to try. It was she, in part, who made it so difficult to return home, both after Eton and most recently. If it weren't for her, he might not have allowed himself to be coaxed into his assignment with the Queen's secret service, something he was determined to see through to the end. He had run away too much, too often in the past, and he had given his word. That matters should resolve into a choice between honoring his word and winning Mira's hand hardly seemed fair.

Yet, in spite of all that was against him, he was determined to succeed. His mother, should one wish to view the matter in the right light, could prove to be the force behind his biggest triumph. It was a fantastic thought, in every way, but he held fast to it through the night and on into the morning. He continued to hold fast to it as he bent over the neck of his horse and made his way to Dover with as much speed as possible, and the thought was with him still when he arrived that evening, stiff and weary, at Cedars, to request from his housekeeper that a tray be brought to his room for his supper.

"And, Mrs. Lambson, as I outlined in my letter, I shall be expecting guests to arrive by this time tomorrow evening. Rather a lot of them, I'm afraid," he added a bit ruefully.

Mrs. Lambson's eyes opened wide, but she gave no other sign that she found his news anything but the stuff of daily fare. "If it pleases my lord, it should be useful to know how many rooms shall be required. I will set about gettin' them aired the moment I have spoken to Mrs. Ward about your dinner."

"Yes, of course," Harry said and reached into his pocket for the list of guests as well as the menus. He held out a bag of coins between his long fingers. "Buy whatever is needed and send someone out to hire extra help come first light."

"Yes, my lord," she said with a bow that was not quick enough to obscure her relief. "And what of your room? I shall send a maid upstairs this very instant."

"That won't be necessary," Harry replied. Heaven knew he had spent the night in places far worse than a room heavy with dust and sporting an unaired bed. Satisfied that all of his wishes would be executed, he turned to make his way up to his room when he heard Mrs. Lambson, in a voice that quavered, ask, "Have I misread this m'lord, or is Lady Avery to be in attendance?"

"Yes, she is. What of it?" he asked, turning to regard her with an expression calculated to put paid to the rebellion he sensed stirred in Mrs. Lambson's breast. As far as Harry knew, the Averys had spent little time at Cedars, however, he owned that one visit was all that was required to leave behind a reputation the villagers would not soon forget.

"It's only that there are some that won't step foot in the house if Lady Avery be in residence, beggin' your pardon, my lord," she said in confirmation of Harry's fears.

"I see," he said shortly in spite of an intense desire to pepper her with questions designed to satisfy his curiosity. "In that case, be on the lookout for families new to town or those with young girls who have never met Lady Avery. And do send the butler up with my tray. You have far too much on your plate already," he added with an acute awareness that Mrs. Lambson's goodwill should prove vital.

"Yes, m'lord," she replied so doubtfully that Harry wondered if perhaps she had the right of it. Perhaps his expectations were a bit unrealistic. Perhaps there was nothing that could be done about the force of nature that was his mother.

Once he had identified a suitable room and shut the door behind him, his mood lifted. All that was needed was some hearty food and a good night's sleep and he would be fit to spend the day preparing to welcome Mira to Cedars. Could it have been less than twenty four hours since he had seen her, since he had held her in his arms and kissed her? It seemed an age and it would be the same numberless hours before he saw her again. He pictured her, the petal-soft skin of her face framed by golden-red curls framing impossibly blue eyes that were fringed with dark lashes above a dainty nose that turned up at the end, highlighting the perfect bow of her mouth—one with lips of satin that tasted like honey . . .

He was startled from his reverie by a knock on the door followed by the entrance of the butler with a tray. Harry hadn't expected anything more than a cold collation of cheese, meat, and bread but he was surprised by the small stack of vellum next to the plate.

"Thank you . . . Randall, is it?" Harry asked. "Have I letters then?"

"Yes on both counts, m'lord," the butler replied and handed them to Harry. "The one with the seal arrived yesterday by special delivery, but the other arrived just moments ago."

With a hollow feeling in the pit of his stomach that had naught to do with hunger, Harry suspected the sealed letter to be his new orders and was relieved to know that George had been nowhere close to Dover when they arrived. He put that aside and opened the other, a plain piece of vellum folded in half, the outside bearing only his name and the inside merely the words: *I know.*

"Who left this?" Harry demanded.

"I couldn't say, m'lord. There was a knock at the door. When I opened it, there was only that—no one on the steps or the street or anywhere that I could see."

"Thank you, Randall," Harry said shortly. He waited until the butler shut the door behind him to break the seal on the second letter. It, like the first, was a study in brevity and contained only the words: *wait for further instructions.* Harry supposed he was meant to wait close to the coast in anticipation of a ship to which he must deliver the letter in his care. He hoped his instructions didn't indicate that a speedy flight from the country was warranted so that he would have a chance to do more in service to his Queen and country.

And what of his other letter? George certainly could have arrived in Dover in time to leave such a note. He had surely read the stolen orders and knew they would send Harry to Dover without delay. George might have been prepared to follow Harry to the coast even before he was himself aware he would be making the journey. The Duke might have even feigned his fit of drunkenness to allow Harry to find his orders; George could hardly follow Harry in the execution of his orders if he had no knowledge of what they contained.

What a fool Harry had been! His first order of business come morning would be to ascertain how long the Duke had been in town. His appetite fled, Harry removed his boots, threw himself on the bed, and emptied his mind of all thoughts but those of Mira.

Within moments he was fully engaged in a slow waltz with his beloved, her lips tantalizingly close to his own and yet impossible to claim on the dance floor. Just as he waltzed the two of them across the imaginary ballroom and through a door to the velvet shadows of the terrace, an ugly thought broke through waves of fatigue and brought him fully awake; what if the note hadn't been left by George? The Duke was weak and easily handled, however, if the missive had been penned by another, there was no way to know to what the author referred—no way to know in which direction danger lurked. It was then that an equally chilling thought occurred to him; Bertie must certainly return.

With a heavy sigh, he rolled out of bed and sat at the table bearing the tray of food. If sleep were to elude him, he would be wise to eat as he pondered his latest predicament. It would be best to reconsider his plans and start anew; only, he had no plans—none at all.

He ate the food and drained the large tankard dry. He pulled out paper and pen and tried to think. He paced the floor, opened the window for fresh air, and paced some more. He opened the door to his bedroom to pace the hall only to come face-to-face with his startled housekeeper in her nightdress and robe who screeched and dropped her candle in the passageway.

"I thought I would collect your tray, m'lord," she murmured and bent to retrieve her candle at the exact moment he did the same. Their heads collided with a loud thunk, and when the stars sprayed across his vision dimmed, he saw that Mrs. Lambson was passed out cold on the passage floor, and there seemed to be a small fire burning in the carpet.

Within seconds, Randall appeared on the landing to see what was amiss. The sight of Mrs. Lambson prostrate on the ground prodded him into action, whereupon he ran to fetch the tankard from Harry's dinner tray and threw the contents onto the promising-looking fire. When no obliging splash of liquid ensued, he turned to give Harry a speaking look.

"I was thirsty," Harry said, feeling unaccountably defensive, then realized the butler meant for him to find another source of water. He ran into his room for the pitcher that sat in the bedside basin; however, the room had not been occupied in years, and the pitcher was dry as the tankard had been.

The taciturn Randall took Mrs. Lambson by the ankles and dragged her away from the growing fire whilst Harry ran up the stairs, calling to the footmen for water, wondering all the while how such a disaster had occurred. If he did not put an end to it, he would be his mother's son indeed.

His anxiety rose until he thought his heart would pound out of his chest, then realized the throbbing in his ears was caused by the footman running down the stairs from their quarters in the attics. Quickly, they set to work: the fire was put out before the smoke became intolerable, and a revived Mrs. Lambson was taken to her room and put to bed with an ice pack for her head. Randall removed the tray from the room and suggested Harry take another down the hall, one not so overcome with fumes.

Harry meekly did as he was told and spent a fitful night. Matters did not improve with the rising of the sun. Everything he set his hand to went awry, and his servants were required to step in time and time again. He grew more and more occupied with the thought that he had inherited his mother's propensity for disaster, most especially when his housekeeper made the sign of the cross every time she removed herself from his presence, a gesture he thought more than a little out of place as Catholic families hardly littered the coastal town of Dover.

Just when he thought he could not abide one more spat between the sisters hired to clean house or another request to change a menu item for a foodstuff Mrs. Lambson found 'more suitable' or report from the butler that a piece of crockery or furniture had been broken yet again, there came the crunch of wheels on gravel that presaged the arrival of a carriage.

Harry assessed the conveyance through the safety of an upstairs window. If it were anyone but the Crenshaws, he would await his guests in the drawing room, as was proper. However, he quickly ascertained that the carriage bore the Crenshaw crest and he headed down the stairs to greet them at the door. He yearned to see Mira but at the moment yearned for her mother, perhaps even more. Lady Crenshaw would certainly put matters to rights in a snap of her fingers, and Harry would be allowed to relax and enjoy his time with his beloved.

Since he first conceived the idea of a party, he had pictured this moment a hundred times: Mira's face alight with a smile as the door opened to reveal her family standing on the step, the softening of her eyes as her gaze fell on Harry just as they had at Haversham House in London, the gentle sway of whatever frippery adorned her hat as she made her way to him, her hands outstretched, her face aglow.

Instead, just as he gained the front hall, the door opened to reveal a distraught and wide-eyed Mira, a flustered Lady Crenshaw, and a rather grim and disheveled Sir Anthony who bore in his arms Harry's supine mother.

He rushed to the door but hardly knew where to look; every pair of eyes, including the closed lids of his mother, registered disaster. He knew, however, that he dared waste no time in recovering his wits; the matter of his mother must be put to rights without delay.

"Mother," he began but was denied the opportunity to say more when Lady Avery's eyes snapped open, and she lifted her head from her faint long enough to say, "I have come at great speed and expense to my health, Herbert, with naught but the clothes on my back, for you must know that one day is not sufficient time to acquire an appropriate wardrobe for such an illustrious event."

The utterance of these simple sentences proved to be too much for she once again fainted dead away and remained lifeless through the transference of her person from Sir Anthony to Harry's waiting arms.

chapter thirteen

Mira could hardly believe what had happened. She had passed nearly two days ensconced in the carriage with her mama and papa and Lady Avery who served only to remind all present that she was sure to be the ruin of any caught in her unfortunate orbit. How was Mira to impress upon her parents that Harry's mother was harmless when she behaved as she did? She had arrived at Prospero Park, unannounced, forced herself into their carriage, insisted that her hosts give up the forward facing seat in favor of herself and Mira, and *would* put her feet, *sans* shoes, in Sir Anthony's lap so he could rub them "as Eustace is wont to do on long journeys." And that was just the outset of their time together.

Mira had fretted the entire way to Dover with regards to what Lady Avery might do next and why Mira's usual calming influence had little effect. She suspected the house party would end in disaster, and that would be the end of her parent's obliging attitude with regards to Harry. At least she knew she was no longer expected to marry George, who thankfully rode to Dover in the Crenshaw crested carriage along with his mother, the Duchess, and Mira's brothers. She did not envy her father the task of disabusing George of the notion their betrothal was nothing more than that.

She absolutely refused to entertain a single thought on the subject of Harry's reaction to his mother's traveling costume, an incredibly voluminous, wide-skirted confection in a garish green that made Mira's head ache. The worst piece of news, however, was Lady Avery's utter lack of luggage whatsoever. What she was to wear throughout her stay at Cedars was a mystery, one which did not bear contemplating.

So adamantly did Lady Avery execute one badly behaved scene after another, Mira might have suspected Harry's mother of purposefully misbehaving in order to put paid to any pretensions of a wedding between her son and Mira, but she knew better; Lady Avery simply *was*. A full two days of hand-clapping, fainting, foot-stamping, pouting, and nonsensical remarks was enough to prove this to Mira in full. By the time they arrived at Cedars, and Lady Avery had feigned a faint whilst being helped out of the carriage by Sir Anthony, forcing him to swoop her into his arms or allow her to split her head open on the carriage steps, Mira saw all her hopes and dreams reduced to ash.

"Ginny, darling," Sir Anthony said as he hefted Lady Avery into his arms, "do take her feet; she is hardly the lithe creature she once was."

Before Mira had a chance to fully examine such a tantalizing remark, Lady Avery rallied. "I will have you know that I am every bit as lithe as ever. Did I not don a gown from my debutante Season for my recent ball?" she asked in bright tones that belied her indisposition nearly as much as the way she kicked at Lady Crenshaw every time she attempted to draw near.

Suddenly, Mira realized everything depended on Harry and his reaction to the scene he was about to witness. She prayed that he would have a few moments to collect himself once he learned of his mother's most recent ailment—that Harry, rather than Bertie, would stride in upon their little tableau and take matters into his capable hands. She imagined an agitated butler and harried housekeeper running hither and yon as they attempted to set matters to rights and how impressed her mama and papa would be once Harry took command of the situation.

With a mingled sense of hope and doom, she took the lead and tripped up the steps to the front door, drew a deep breath, and knocked. It was opened by the butler, who, by rights, should have anticipated their arrival and made himself available for whatever was needed, from the collecting of luggage to the transportation of a swooned Lady Avery, but he did not. Instead, he merely looked at them, his expression one of abject horror the moment his gaze fell upon Harry's mother.

And then Mira saw Harry—*her* Harry—the one she needed right this very moment. She wanted nothing more than to throw herself into his arms and pour out her tale of woe, however, by the time his mother had made the deficiencies in her wardrobe known, Mira could see that Harry guessed all. Without a moment's hesitation, he took Lady Avery from Sir Anthony's arms and stood her on her own two feet. She crumpled a bit, and Mira thought she must go down, but the volume of what could not be less than three petticoats under her horrid green skirt kept her aloft.

"Now, Mother, this must stop. You are a grown woman, and that is what is needed in my hostess. I cannot depend on you if you are to faint dead away at every breath of wind."

"Of course, Herbert," she replied with what Mira felt to be genuine gumption. "It's only that I am so very warm. I believe I must have donned one too many petticoats."

Over Lady Avery's head, Mira's and Harry's gazes met in a moment of pure accord. Very carefully, Mira angled a foot to quickly lift the green skirt without calling attention to her actions, one which revealed nearly half a dozen wide-hooped petticoats, as well as several day dresses, a pair of ball gowns, both blue, a night rail, and a riding habit. How Lady Avery had kept this superfluity of fabric from the notice of her fellow travelers was astonishing to say the least.

"Lady Avery," Mira suggested as mildly as her sudden panic allowed, "the color in your cheeks is quite high. "Perhaps you should lie down. Let us find your room while the housekeeper sends up a maid to make you more comfortable."

"Thank you," Harry replied, "I think that an excellent notion. Mother, I suggest you demonstrate your appreciation for Miss Crenshaw's kindness by indulging her every wish."

"I shall inform Mrs. Lambson that a maid is required," the butler intoned and he hurried off just as Mira led Lady Avery up the stairs. Mira, glad of a reason to draw her parents' attention away from Harry's mother in favor of her son, hoped he was doing his utmost to ensure her mother's and father's comfort after their ordeal. It meant so much to Mira to know that she might rightly rely on Harry to see her parents settled which left her free to see to Lady Avery. Once Mira donned the peevish Lady Avery in something light and airy, Mira felt confident that Harry's mother would be a new woman.

However, once they obtained a satisfactory bedchamber, Mira could not resist satisfying her curiosity. "Lady Avery, why don so much clothing at once? she asked with a gesture that took in Lady Avery from head to toe. "Why forsake luggage in favor of making yourself a literal clotheshorse?"

"Oh, you clever girl, you have caught on to my little deception! Still, you have so much to learn," Lady Avery said with a knowing look. "If you can't acquire the trick of making a proper entrance, you shall never be deemed a lady."

"I'm afraid I still cannot fathom . . ." Mira demurred as she helped Lady Avery step out of her skirt. "I am persuaded a true lady makes a regal entrance with much attention paid to decorum and self-restraint."

"That is what the haughty duchesses and their husbands' snide mistresses would have you think. The truth is, a *soupcon* of drama goes a long way!"

"I am persuaded you are correct upon that score," Mira assured her whilst she privately mused on what terrible misfortune had caused Lady Avery's definition of 'a bit' to wander so far from that of the dictionary.

"Of course you do, darling girl! So you must perceive how delicious it was to enter Cedars swooned in the arms of a man who was not my husband and fully prepared to make such a speaking remark!"

"By 'speaking remark,' I imagine you refer to the one you made with regards to hastening to join your son without stopping to pack your things," Mira suggested as she peeled away several layers of those things from Lady Avery's increasingly thinner form.

"I knew you would understand! And when Herbert marries you, I hope you shall take a page from my book and make your wedding one none shall ever forget. I know I intend to," she said with an arch smile so full of perverse promise that Mira felt her knees turn to water and was forced to sit on the edge of the bed.

"But . . . why?" Mira asked, her hopes turned once more to ashes.

"Why what?" Lady Avery replied, bright as a summer afternoon and happily occupied with the task of clothing removal.

"Why would you wish to draw so much attention to yourself at your own son's wedding?"

"Because it shall be such a spectacular day! The more important the event, the more drama is required, that is what I always say, for you see, I never had a wedding; Eustace and I eloped," she added with a sad, little moue. "As such, I have been plotting and planning every detail of Herbert's nuptials since the day he was born. I have even done up a dozen sketches of his bride's gown. It is the dearest thing positively groaning under the weight of hundreds of satin roses attached hither and yon! However," she added with a decidedly downcast air, "I must admit, I am at a loss as to this house party. I've barely had time to breathe, let alone think. Perhaps you might help me plan something perfect for tonight!" she asked with a flurry of claps.

"I imagine you shall do well enough on your own," Mira said faintly.

"I suppose you are right. A penchant for drama is one of my God-given gifts; I defy anyone to deny it," she said with a sigh that denoted a resignation towards her deific burden.

Mira could think of no reply that suited such a statement and longed for escape. What had become of the maid whose arrival would release Mira from her duty? How long before she was able to quit the room without giving offense? Was there time to gather her parents and flee the premises before Lady Avery unveiled her preposterousness, her next plot, or, heaven prevent, any part of her person?

Finally, Lady Avery was down to her corset and pantaloons, the high color in her cheeks had receded, and Mira felt she could, in good conscience, leave Lady Avery to her own devices. Since it was clear to Mira that Lady Avery, happily occupied at the dressing table, would hardly notice anything beyond her own reflection in the looking-glass, Mira departed without even a by-your-leave.

As she walked down the stairs to the front hall, her head splitting with unpleasant possibilities, the front door opened to reveal Stephen and Adrian, loaded down with an astonishing amount of baggage.

"Oh!" Mira cried, delighted to have additional reminders of home to bolster her in what had proved to be trying circumstances. She flew down the stairs to greet them but was startled by the sight of Her Grace, George's mother, still styled as the Duchess of Marcross until such time her son should take a wife. Mira, painfully aware that she was, in George's and his mother's eyes, the girl poised for such a position, did not wonder at the frown on Her Grace's face when she looked up to see her intended successor. The Duchess was a beautiful woman and still somewhat young; doubtless she did not look forward to a journey through life as the dowager duchess.

The butler and several footman were soon on hand to divest Mira's brothers from what proved to be mostly Her

Grace's bags, and it was not long before Harry appeared to greet the newcomers.

"But I do not see His Grace!" Harry said in tones more than a little reminiscent of Bertie. "Is he not with you?"

The Duchess responded with naught but a roll of her eyes.

"Miss Crenshaw," Harry said, turning to address her, "I'm afraid you must enlighten me. Does the roll of the eyes indicate that her son *is* with her but out, perhaps seeing to the rubbing down of the horses, or that he is presently a resident of the lunatic asylum?" he asked with a giddy giggle. "For, you must know, I have long thought it the best option for a case such as his."

Mira was more than a little impressed at the Duchess's utter lack of response, but Stephen's and Adrian's arrested expressions clearly revealed their discomfort at Harry's lack of decorum. At the same time, she suspected this was a breach of manners of which even Stephen could approve.

"His Grace set out with us in the carriage," Adrian explained, "but shortly thereafter took the journey alone on his mount."

"An unnatural son," announced his mother, who was engaged with the removal of her hat and gloves precisely as if the front hall were her personal dressing room. "I have never understood him," she added with a sharp look for Mira.

"I am persuaded he is cognizant of his duty to his position," Mira began but soon faltered. There was no response to the Duchess's remark that seemed other than impertinent.

"Your Grace," Harry intoned with an exaggerated bow. "I have been remiss in my duties and must tender my apologies.

Miss Crenshaw," he said as he took her elbow and steered her towards the double doors leading into the parlor, "allow me to find you a seat by the fire in the faultless company of your esteemed parents."

Mira, her back now turned to the Duchess, could only wonder as to the effect of Harry's neglect upon George's mother, however, her response was far from what she could have expected.

"Ah, so that is where you have hidden him," the Duchess purred, whereupon she pushed her way past Mira and opened the double doors without the aid of so much as a single footman. "Tony!" she cried and took herself on winged feet across the room where Mira's father and mother recovered from their journey.

Mira turned to Harry to decipher his reaction and was shocked to learn he was not in the least surprised. "You knew of this warm relationship between my father and his aunt?"

"I should hardly call it warm," Harry said with a look for her father who leaped to his feet and ran through the door to the gardens for all the world like Joseph from Pharaoh's wife. With far more grace, Lady Crenshaw also rose, a determined smile fixed to her face, and held out her hand to the Duchess in greeting. The Duchess had no choice but to greet Lady Crenshaw in return, and the two of them were soon seated across from one another on the sofa, prepared to do battle.

"Someone ought to rescue her," Stephen suggested.

"If only Her Grace weren't a woman," Adrian carped as he pounded a fist into his hand.

"I am astounded!" Mira said. "I hadn't the slightest idea there was anything between them and yet you two have known all along?"

"There's naught between them," Adrian insisted. "She simply wishes there were, that is all."

"Why has she been invited, anyway?" Stephen demanded.

"It was needful," Harry said shortly. "Go and see if you can't find her another post to scratch at," he added with a nod at Stephen and Adrian. "There is something I would say to Mira before we join you."

The conspiratorial smile on Adrian's face was at odds with Stephen's obvious reluctance to fall in with Harry's plan, but they soon disappeared into the parlor and shut the doors behind them.

"Finally, we are alone," Mira said and smiled, though she knew her lips trembled so that they betrayed her misgivings. It would never do for someone to walk through the great hall, alive with sunshine from the mullioned windows, to witness them alone and deep in conversation, or worse, in kisses, if Mira had her wish.

"Yes," Harry said, and turned to face her, his expression grave. "It is, in part, with regard to our time alone I wish to speak." He took her hands in his, warming them, though, until that moment, she had not realized they were cold. "I believe I have made my feelings known beyond any doubt, however, I was wrong to expect your feelings to mirror mine. I should not have forced myself upon you."

"I have been kissed but thrice, my lord," Mira said, her trepidation flown, "each by the same man. If it pleases you, I would point out that I slapped you but twice."

Mira felt the fluttering of her stomach increase in accordance with the width of Harry's smile, and it was glorious.

"If by that I am to assume my kisses are welcome until I feel the sting of your palm against my cheek," he said with a squeeze of her fingers, "I think perhaps I should not risk it."

Mira cocked her head and gave him an impudent smile. "I cannot credit it! You have always been a taker of risks, Harry Haversham."

"You speak truer than you know," he said, his expression once again grave. "But there are things . . . people, rather, whom I shall not risk. This is why I feel it needful to warn you that Bertie might . . . no," he said with a shake of his head, "*must* make an appearance."

Mira opened her mouth to protest but was thwarted by the finger he laid against her lips. "I do not know from which direction hazard lurks and if I am found out . . . that is to say, if my secret is revealed, all who are close to me will be in danger. However, none will believe Bertie conversant enough with a pistol to cock it, leave alone pull the trigger."

Mira had much to say, the least of which was not a decided aversion towards the brandishing of pistols, cocked or otherwise, and attempted to convey such in spite of his finger against her lips, but he would have none of it.

"My darling, I do not speak idly. If I am to lose you as my wife, so be it, if it means I have guarded well your life."

Mira felt her eyes grow wide with amazement. She knew Harry was possessed of imperative reasons for his actions and trusted him even when she most likely should not; however, this was beyond anything she had presumed. All in all, she was left with very little to say but say it she would. "I understand, but, oh, Harry, how I wish it were not so!"

He dropped his hand and pulled her close to take her quickly into his arms. "Another thing I dare not risk is your parents' ire. Should we be discovered behaving thus, your good father could prove the most dangerous of all."

Mira nodded in agreement but could not imagine her papa would willingly hurt Harry, regardless of the cause. She took a step back and tried to smile. "It's only that I have so longed for your presence, not only since we last met, but for these past four years." She felt the tears gather in her throat and she choked a bit. "Harry, I have missed you so!"

His reply was swallowed up by the turning of wheels in the gravel drive and the approach of the butler in response. Quickly, Harry pulled her deep into the shadow of the stair. "Meet me in the stables at daybreak. I will have a horse saddled for you and we shall go for a ride before the other guests awake."

Mira found it easy to smile to this, and then Harry was off to greet his newest arrived visitors.

By evening, all of the guests had arrived, George not excepted, though his absence until time to dress for dinner went unexplained. Mira greeted him with a degree of pleasure not one whit less than she had received all of Harry's guests but refused to allow him any claim on her above that of cousins. It was not her place to correct George as to his pretensions to her hand in marriage; that was a chore best left to her father. However, she refused to behave as if the Duke were her suitor, even when at risk of stirring his wrath. Once she had retired to her room to dress for dinner and distractions were few, her attention turned to what Harry's mother might have planned for the hours and days to come. Mira's stomach knotted at the thought and wondered if she shouldn't simply claim a sick headache and take to her bed until morning. However, she knew Harry counted on her to help diminish the impact of his mother's antics, as well as those of Bertie, should he make an appearance.

In this she was not disappointed.

chapter fourteen

Harry knew himself to be grateful his mother had remained out of sight until dinner. He *told* himself he was grateful she had found time to act as his hostess in spite of having been occupied with he knew not what all afternoon. He *felt* he should be grateful for her hand-clapping and artless conversation as well, for it smoothed the way for Harry to be seen in the same repugnant light. He never needed to play the fool more than now for he had received another ominous note under his door as he dressed for dinner. Try as he might, however, he could find nothing for which to be grateful with regards to the dead and dying fish that lined the center of his dinner table.

He hardly knew how to react, nor, it seemed, did his alter ego, Bertie. He stood at the head of the table and gaped along with his guests while his mother clapped and curtsied like an actress at a curtain call. "*Maman,* what is this?" he twittered a la Bertie, the memory of his most recent message heavy on his mind. It read: *Her fate is sealed,* and could only have been penned by someone in the house, one who most likely watched the fish flop about in their shallow graves even now.

"Why, Herbert, you know how much I wished for fish at our last do. And, yes, I do know why you are doubtful. The fish should have been in a bit more water. I can't think why the servants did not choose deeper bowls! I am persuaded Prinny used deeper bowls for *his* fish."

Harry drew a deep breath, exchanged a glance with Mira who stood down-table with her wide-eyed parents, and brayed with laughter. "Poor *Maman*! Those fish were but tiny, imported carp, not English sole, and they swam down table in a miniature river of his own devising, not bowls from the scullery!" He followed this with another bout of laughter that bent him in half before wildly waving his arms at his guests to indicate that they should be seated.

To his great relief, everyone sat in spite of the oppressive double-eyed stare from the dead sole. He took advantage of the general hubbub to instruct the footman behind his chair to have the poor creatures removed.

"But, Herbert, I hadn't time for imported fish," she murmured. "You will spoil everything!"

"I'm afraid it's a sight too late for that," he said in low tones designed to keep his words from the ears of the Crenshaws halfway down table. "Tell me the fish is your only surprise for the evening."

"I could say so, but I'm not entirely sure it wouldn't be a lie," Lady Avery said with a pout.

"Oh Mother, you are such an original!" Harry roared with laughter in spite of the pointed indifference of the assemblage at large who were all engaged in their own, doubtless, far less compelling conversations.

"Well, I do try, Herbert," she riposted, mollified. "But I must admit I am dubious as to how I shall carry off the zoo."

"Zoo?" Harry echoed as he gazed down the table at his beloved and bid her a silent *adieu.*

"Well, one can hardly call it a whole zoo when all I have managed to round up is the monkey, but, mark my words, I shall have a full zoo not many days hence."

Harry methodically spooned soup into his mouth and wondered how one divests oneself of a monkey whilst working on how to act like one without alienating the Crenshaws. Another glance down the table revealed to him a puzzled Adrian, an angry Stephen, their tearful mother and distraught father, and a white-faced Mira. The Duke and his mother, the Duchess, wore the self-same expression, one of smug satisfaction. How Harry longed to wipe the prim smile from George's face with his fist but knew it would only add to his quickly expanding list of troubles.

He focused, instead, on his planned morning ride with Mira and took comfort in the fact that one little monkey was a good deal less trouble than an elephant, should his mother devise a means to obtain one. The fact she had not, as of yet, meant naught.

The remainder of the evening passed in a blur of a badly behaved Lady Avery, an obnoxious Bertie, and the domination of the Crenshaws by George and his mother who, between them, allowed no one else near enough to Mira and her family to exchange a single word. Consigning his guests to flames of his mother's lack of decorum, Harry retired early in a foul temper.

With morning came a reluctant clarity. The likelihood that he would lose Mira, either through his mother's antics or his own, was perilously great. A period to his existence might even be in order, if those who sought his life had their wishes. Briefly, he contemplated the most likely instrument of his demise and shuddered at the raft of possibilities. He had already been shot at, but there were other means available to anyone who stayed under the same roof, as Harry suspected he must.

There came a rap at the door, and he jumped out of bed to answer, forgetful that he still wore only his nightshirt. The opened door thankfully revealed only the butler with a red-sealed missive in his hand.

"This has just arrived," he intoned as he handed the note over to his master.

Harry took it and shut the door without a word. Hastily, he split the red wax seal that kept his orders safe from prying eyes and, with a sense of finality he felt deep in the marrow of his bones, read that he was to row out from a secluded cove along the shore to board ship and deliver to its captain the sealed missive in Harry's possession. It would seem he were to take a journey as well, for he was to stay aboard, leading Harry to wonder if the possibility of his identity having been compromised might have reached his superiors. The fact that he was to leave before next light came as a crushing blow.

Harry was aware of three things straight away. One, his immediate danger was worse than he had supposed and every person with whom he shared a roof, including Mira, could potentially catch a stray bullet, consume a poisoned *Poisson*, or possibly even share his fate as he fell to his death down the stairs. Two, he must add the task of procuring a dinghy, getting it ready for his use and hidden, to his list for the day, one which already included the purging of a monkey, as well as any other creatures his mother managed to corral in the meantime, and without anyone the wiser. Three, he must make the most of his morning ride with Mira as it was likely the last moments they would spend alone together. His heart faltered at the thought, but he owned Mira was never truly meant for one such as he and never had been. He had disqualified himself from the honor with his actions, and there was nothing left for him to do but restore her to a life of peace and safety.

Hastily, he dressed for riding but not before he crumbled the wax seal into tiny pieces and burnt the message on the fire. Suddenly, he wondered what had become of his last red-sealed missive, the one delivered by the butler the night of his arrival. He conducted a search of his room but it was not to be found; either someone had taken it—someone such as George or whomever was the author of the anonymous notes—or Harry had burned it as he should have. However, try as he might, he could not recall doing so.

Eager to join Mira for their ride, he forced himself to concentrate and was rewarded with a clear picture of the red-sealed orders where they lay on the tray Randall had brought up, the same tray he had thereafter removed. Harry realized that the fire on the landing had distracted him from his vigilance, and that the orders had not been burnt but had been taken down to the kitchens where they might have fallen into any number of hands. He was grateful that those particular orders divulged little more than that Harry was to stay put, but their presence alone was additional proof that Harry was far from the fribble he affected to be. Grateful that his most recent orders had not fallen under the eyes of his enemies, he took up his pistol and departed his bedchamber, leery of anyone who might forestall him and thus deprive him of even one precious minute with Mira.

As he did not wish to wake any of his guests and encourage unwanted company, both congenial and murderous, Harry waited to don his boots until he gained the front hall. He handled the great front door with as much care as possible and hoped few to none heard the slight squeak of the hinges. Finally, he gained the stables and was delighted to see Mira had arrived before him. She was glorious in her deep blue riding habit, her hair aglow in a rare morning beam of sunshine, and the way she smiled and held her hands out to him induced such a wash of emotion—love, adoration, regret, sorrow, and longing—that tears started in his eyes.

Abashed that she should see his weakness or perhaps discern his latest secret, he shook away the drops of moisture and affected pain from an imaginary bit of straw before he took her hands in his and smiled in return.

Quickly, he saddled the horses. "Are you ready then?" he asked, just as he always had when they had ridden together as youngsters. He knew she recalled it as well when she tossed her fiery mane of gold-red curls and answered as she always had in days gone by.

"When am I not?" The saucy smile that accompanied this piece of impertinence was thoroughly familiar, but the sidelong look from beneath her long lashes and the blush that followed were entirely new. With a wide grin that belied the constriction of his heart, he cupped his hands to facilitate her dainty foot and, just as he had done so many times before, tossed her into the saddle.

They guided their horses into the path that divided a nearby copse of ancient cedars and trotted for quite some time in amicable silence. Harry wanted to say so much but cast aside one precarious topic of conversation after another; since Mira didn't seem any more disposed to talk, he remained silent. He attempted to enjoy the squeak of the leather, the scent of the leaves, the breeze in his hair, but only the warmth of her gaze could touch him. In spite of the light and bright air, redolent of the sea and abrim with birdsong, his oppression was so great it threatened to collapse his lungs. To remain so close at her side and yet so far from his heart's desire was a torture he could bear no longer.

With a cry of frustration, he pressed his feet into his mount, rode ahead a pace or two, and swung his horse round to face Mira. He could see that she was startled but he chose not to pause long enough for speech. Instead, he urged his horse alongside hers so that his right knee grazed her left, turned in the saddle, and pulled her into his arms.

With a sigh, she rested her head against his chest where she doubtless felt every beat of his thundering heart. It was then he knew she had guessed the truth of his imminent departure, yet she did not complain or lament or even speak. He had loved her as a girl, had loved her more when he saw the young lady she had become, but he thought he should never love anyone as much as this woman in his arms who trusted him so far beyond what he deserved.

He longed to kiss her before it was too late, fearing it would be their last; the thought served to remind him that she belonged not to him but some other man who would one day make her his wife. He prayed he had said enough to dissuade her from granting George that honor but owned the identity of her husband was no longer his affair. His horse took a step back, and he was forced to release her.

However, once she had regained her seat, he took her face in his hands and willed her to know what he would do if he were free to do so. She stared back at him, her heart in her eyes, and with a little cry, put her hands up to cover his and pressed her lips to the heel of his hand.

They remained thus until Harry became aware of the presence of other horses, presumably with riders. He grasped the reins and wheeled his horse in the direction of the threat just as George and his mother emerged from behind a stand of trees. It flashed through Harry's mind to wonder how much they had seen and, for Mira's sake, was gratified he had not kissed her after all. He must ever after consider the kisses they shared at Haversham House as both the promise for the future they implied, as well as their farewell.

"Well, well, well," George said. "It would seem we were not the first to rise with the dawn this morning."

The Duchess, her heavy, honey-gold hair twisted into elaborate knots under a brown hat that matched her eyes, sniffed and looked away as if Harry and Mira were the very least of her concerns. Harry, suddenly aware that his enemy could be a woman as well as a man, heartily hoped they were.

"Why, Miss Crenshaw, it is His Grace and Her Grace!" Harry squealed. "One might almost refer to them as The Graces if there weren't only the two of them." He added a pithy laugh that sounded sharp in his own ears and wheeled his restive mount around in a circle to address George and his mother yet again. "How fortunate that you have arrived! I was just telling Miss Crenshaw how I must be off to see my tailor. He isn't what one would hope for in London but he does well enough for these backwater affairs."

George cocked a brow in question and drawled, "I am shocked to learn you employ a London tailor. I had thought *all* of your affairs to be of a backwater nature."

Harry felt his skin bloom red with anger and his jaw clench until he could hear the grinding of his teeth above the Duchess's unladylike laughter. However, until Harry sailed away, Bertie must needs hold the reins.

"I should think that most of Lord Haversham's wardrobe to have been made abroad, "Mira asked in mild tones designed to soothe. "You are always the epitome of elegance, Lord Haversham, even if Papa feels you sometimes eschew lace to your detriment."

"Oh," Harry said with a crow of laughter. "It is my manner of dress His Grace refers to, is it? Well, color me contrite!" he quipped with a bow so deep he was in danger of poking his eye out on the pommel.

"You are far more remarkable than I had remembered," the Duchess commented with a smile more snide than unctuous. "How could I have forgotten such a wit as yours?"

"Did you hear that, Miss Crenshaw?" Harry twittered. "She thinks me a wit, a speaker of *bon mots*, a purveyor of mental delicacies! Have you heard the one about the fan? Or was it the flute? I hardly can remember!"

"We have heard it," George muttered. "Several times at dinner last night and at least once before if my memory serves me right."

Harry felt Mira's gaze on him and knew she wished to share one of her mirthful glances, but he dared not. "Then I shall not trouble you with another rendering. At least not until luncheon!" he said with a hearty bray. "I am off then, to my tailor, as I have so said. *A bientot, alor*s!"

he called and rode off as clumsily as could manage. He paused and turned to giddily wave a handkerchief and thereby verify that Mira had ridden off with her aunt and cousin as her knew her to be safer in their company than at his own side.

The knowledge sobered him as he felt something akin to despair rise in his breast. Only once before had he been in so hopeless a position. Though the boating accident had happened four years prior, it was just one more matter that stood in the way of his happiness with Mira. Now he was England and operating in her very orbit, he had long believed that could never occur. Perhaps he was capable of formulating the words to tell her the truth about what had happened that long ago night after all.

With great effort, he gathered his wits and told himself that as long as both he and Mira were alive and not wed to another, there was still a chance they could be together. His first priority must be safety, and his second to get through the remainder of the day without incident. Once he was out at sea, he could worry about all that stood between them; her parents' objections, his hopeless mother, the possibility that Mira might wed another, his own doubts and fears and feelings of unworthiness—but not before.

When he reached the great lawn that stretched between Cedars and the path down to the sea, he urged his horse into a gallop and streaked to the stables. There was much to do, but first, he must catch his mother's monkey. A rapid but thorough investigation of the stables produced a net on a pole that had most likely been used, quite recently in fact, for the scooping of fish from the sea. Something told Harry he would have a far more difficult time in the capture of the monkey than even his mother had in the acquisition of the sole at table the night prior.

He could just see her, barefoot, her skirts hitched up between her legs as she dragged the net wildly through the water, and finally, the stamp of her foot at her failure, eventual acknowledgment of defeat, and her return to the house to order some poor unsuspecting servant to fetch her fish. The fact that he could so easily picture such a scene threatened to renew his feelings of despair, but he ruthlessly quashed it and commenced his hunt.

He thought the best place to start would be in the house, though he could hardly corner his mother in full view of his guests and demand from her the monkey's whereabouts. It would be best if he found it on his own, unobserved by any of his visitors, most of whom should have risen from their beds by now. As such he went round to the back of the house and entered through the kitchen door.

"Heaven have mercy!" squawked the cook as she waved a wooden spoon at him. "You gave me such a turn!"

"I am sorry to have disturbed you, only, I must ask . . . it sounds utterly absurd, I know, but have you seen a monkey hereabouts?"

"A monkey! A real live monkey?" she cried. "I should think not. Not in my kitchen!" she insisted with a warning look for the various kitchen girls who ranged round her and who might, unaccountably, be hiding a monkey somewhere about their persons.

"Ah, well, you never know when monkey brains might appear on the menu," he said.

"Monkey brains for eating? I have never heard of such a thing!" the cook cried and shooed him out of the room.

His hunt through the breakfast room was deplete of monkeys but filled with more guests that he had expected, among them the entire Crenshaw clan, as well as Mira's closest friend, Viola Carlson-Johnson. If the way she bent her head in earnest conversation with Stephen was any indication, she was fast on her way to becoming Mira's sister-in-law as well.

"What is that deplorable object you have there, my lord?" Lucy Sutherland asked. "It reeks to high heaven!"

"Oh, this?" Harry said. "It's . . . . a butterfly net. I have a mind to catch a few this morning," he added with a Bertie-like twitter designed to remove the suspicion from every face in the room. In point of fact, he had never seen so many pairs of quizzical eyes in all his life. Only too late did he ascertain the presence of his mother.

"Oh, don't be silly, Herbert! That's the net I used to catch fish yesterday. It is quite broken, I am sure! If fish won't swim into it, I am persuaded the butterflies will simply fly away from such a noxious thing, aren't you?" she asked of Sir Hollis who was too busy scrutinizing Harry to respond.

In fact, the Carlson-Johnsons as well as the Sutherlands, the Marquess and his daughter Ramona, and the DiPastenas were all staring at Harry with a disconcerting intensity. The thought that any one of them could have something to do with the notes left under his door unnerved him so that he almost dropped the net as he stumbled from the room. Thankfully, he left before his mother had the chance to bring up the subject of monkeys or zoos or what she might have in store for the ball later that night. Whatever it was, he had no time to worry about it at present.

The drawing room was littered with various other guests, none of whom bore the expression of one who had encountered a monkey on the premises, so he headed upstairs and looked through his mother's rooms in her absence. His search turned up nothing but a few mice, and, with great reluctance, he decided his time was better spent in the hunt for a small rowboat to plant in readiness for the night.

This chore was child's play compared to the last, and he returned across the lawn to the house in time to witness Mira's return from her ride, along with the Duke and Duchess and several other guests who had attached themselves to their party at some point along the way. In contrast to his expectations, Mira did not sulk or wilt; she seemed hardy and happy to be in the company of others. Not for the first time it occurred to him that she was better off with someone—anyone—other than himself. Though he was sure she knew that he must once again bow out of her life, he could not be so confident that she would forgive him. However, a man who harbored dark secrets, heavy obligations, and the Haversham genes was hardly what a young girl dreamed of in a husband. If he were honest, he barely wanted it for her either.

Rather than join Mira in the stables as he wished to do, he sheered off, determined to busy himself with other tasks. He had invited a number of gentlemen in expectations that, should Harry not win the Crenshaws' approval, one or two would prove more palatable to Mira than George. It could hardly be otherwise. Until then Harry would make himself least in sight until dinner which would give Mira a chance at privacy with a suitable candidate for her hand and afford Harry a much needed rest from the burden that was Bertie.

Though his insistence on visiting his tailor was meant to be a ruse, Harry's despondent mood was hardly lightened by the suit of clothes he donned for the night. Unlike his London wardrobe, his clothing at Cedars had not been updated in quite some time, and the seams of the slightly too-small suit he had brought with him had finally succumbed to the pressure of Harry's more mature body. This meant he must resort to a suit that was too short, too narrow, and too out of date to feel the least elegant. He loathed that Mira's last sight of him would include far too much shirtsleeve and silken hose for his liking, but there was naught to be done about it.

Dinner passed in wave after wave of misery, and halfway through Harry was unable to take another bite. He sat in silence and picked at his napkin while he studied the faces at table in an attempt to determine who was most likely to be a traitor to his, or even her, country. His gaze strayed to Mira more often than was seemly, but the sight of her exquisite face entirely devoid of any sign she mourned his departure was too painful to endure for many minutes in a row.

Harry felt his head droop lower and his chin sink deeper into his cravat, but he was too dispirited to rouse himself. It was with relief that he quit the table without lingering with a glass of port as did the other men. Instead, he employed his time until the dancing to renew his hunt for the monkey. An active search soon devolved into a mere wandering of the halls while he punished himself with one pessimistic thought after another, most of them having to do with Mira's demeanor. Perhaps he had been wrong to think she loved him. She did not seem to suffer as did he and, after all, she had never said as much.

He commenced the ball by asking Mira's friend, Miss Carlson-Johnson, to dance. He hoped his actions would not be misconstrued, but he refused to give his would-be-murderer the impression that he was overly attached to any one young lady. To do so would be to put her in danger, so he followed up the first dance with a waltz with Lucy, a jig with Heather, the March with Ramona, and the Quadrille with Jenny. He was acutely aware he had but a few hours more in Mira's presence, perhaps forever, but he spent the second hour of the ball in the company of his other guests as well, and he took Viola Carlson-Johnson into midnight supper on his arm for good measure.

He could not enjoy his folly, however, especially when every time he met Mira's gaze, she stared back at him with smiling eyes. Hardly knowing what he wanted—Mira safe or in his arms—he sent Viola back to the ballroom on the arm of a disgruntled Stephen. Harry watched them go, begrudging them their straight and simple path to marriage. He watched Mira go as well, on the arm of one of the gentlemen he had invited for her benefit, and waited until the room emptied of his guests while he sat alone and attempted to gain a semblance of control over his emotions. It was then that he thought he saw, out of the corner of his eye, an ominous shadow scurry across the room. He was on his feet in an instant, and the pistol he always kept concealed in his clothing was out in a flash. However, there was no one in the room.

Carefully, his pistol still aloft, Harry bent to regard what lay below the tablecloth and spied a pair of very short and hairy legs hanging down from a chair on the opposite side. He threw himself across the cluttered table only to be met by a wide-eyed stare from a pair of huge brown eyes set above two rows of very sharp teeth which moved up and down in unison with the most appalling screeching Harry had ever had occasion to hear.

He threw out his free hand to throttle his mother's monkey, but it bounded off the chair and down to the far end of the table where Harry regarded it from his position sprawled across the remains of someone's meal. He knew the moment he stood the monkey would be off again and decided it was a pointless endeavor. Thoroughly frustrated, Harry got to his feet and replaced his pistol as the monkey jumped to the floor and disappeared under a chair. With a sigh of disgust, he dropped into the nearest seat and put his face in his hands. If his mother wished to entertain a monkey, who was he to say her nay? If Lord Melbourne wished him to depart England, how could he refuse? If Mira failed to go into a decline over his departure, so be it!

With the resignation of the damned, he removed the remains of someone's dinner from his shirtfront and walked to the door, determined to spend his last hour in England with whomever was willing. To his mingled dismay and delight, his way was barred by the one person he least expected to see.

chapter fifteen

"Why, I doubt I have seen anything so comical!" Mira said blithely. She could not help but notice Harry's low spirits at dinner and ached to see him smile. "I believe you have a sprig of parsley in your hair, just there." She pointed to the offensive article, but despite the care she took to make light of it, his face drained white and his eyes glittered in a way that wrung her heart.

She took a step closer and put her hand on his arm. "There is a waltz playing; I don't believe we have danced together all night," she added breezily as if she hadn't suffered agonies from his neglect of her. She couldn't fathom why he should wish to dance with every girl but she; it couldn't be that he was put off by her appearance as she had taken care with her toilette and donned a gown in his favorite deep blue that matched her eyes to perfection.

Harry said nothing, nor did he move, and, in spite of their being quite alone in the room, there came a strange sound from behind him on the table. She stepped round him to see what it could be and gasped in surprise. "Harry, is that a monkey I see?"

Finally, he stirred and to her relief, spoke. "Yes, I do believe it is."

"Well," she said, determined to have her waltz, monkey or no. "I don't see how it should prevent our dancing together."

She thought he bit back a smile, but the slight curving of his cheek prodded a tear to spill down his face and the ghost of the smile was gone. Thoroughly at a loss, she reached up to pluck the greenery from his hair, but he anticipated her action and threw up a hand to forestall her.

The misery that had threatened to overwhelm her all day rose into her chest but she waited, her hand held painfully tight in his own. Finally, he opened his eyes, his brow creased with sadness or anger, she knew not which. Mira longed to know what she had done to displease him, but it seemed that his store of words was used up.

"I shan't mind the parsley if you do not," she said, choking on tears of her own.

Suddenly, the monkey took up a shrill screaming so loud it threatened to bring others into the supper room and put an end to their privacy. Mira was crushed. The moment she had seen his face in the stables earlier that morning, she had known he must leave but knew not when and assumed they would spend every possible moment together in the meantime. She had been at pains to hide her sorrow so as not to spoil what time they had together but to no avail; he had stayed away all day, had taken supper with her best friend, and had failed to ask Mira for even one dance the entire evening. What had she done to deserve such pointed disdain? How long did they have together before he disappeared from her life yet again?

It seemed not long, for the moment the inquisitive faces of his guests began to flood into the room, Harry pushed through them and stalked through the doorway. Mira watched him go with her heart in her throat, unable to follow or speak or even think.

"Is that . . . a monkey?" the Marquess asked. "Because, if it is, I know of a very good recipe for monkey brain stew."

Mira felt a frown crease her own face as she turned to face him. "People eat monkey brains?"

"Not Sarah Siddons!" Lady Avery cried as she forced her way through the crowd hovering around the entrance to the room. "Oh, Miss Crenshaw! I most especially wanted you to meet Sarah, my monkey. I had hoped to have an entire zoo set up for tonight, but even if I could have found an animal other than a mangy old bear, I wasn't terribly clear on where I should have it. I thought perhaps in that corner . . ." she mused as if Mira's world were not crashing to the ground.

For once in her life Mira was glad of her brothers' advice and happily ignored her hostess who was too caught up with fashioning a cage for Sarah Siddons from the dining chairs to notice Mira's neglect. Hastily, she made her way out of the supper room through the gathering crowd that included slack-jawed Crenshaws of every stamp. The exception was her mother who smiled her encouragement and put out a hand to halt Mira's progress and whisper in her ear.

"It was when I had run from a house party that your father followed *me*," she said with a squeeze to Mira's hand who threw her arms about her mother for a tight embrace.

"Oh, Mama! Thank you!" she cried, whereupon she ran into the ballroom and looked about for Harry. It took but a moment to determine he was not there and she struggled to tamp down her burgeoning sense of alarm. Why had she never told him of her feelings? If he were to leave her again, it wouldn't, *couldn't* be before she had told him how very much she loved him. She attempted to work out where he might have gone as she ran through the door leading out of the ballroom into the passage and down the stairs that led to the main floor of the house.

Once arrived at the ground floor, she heard a faint commotion that seemed to be coming from the back of the house. Breathless and nearly frantic, she rushed through a maze of passages and finally into the kitchen to find the servant girls cowered in the corner like so many birds in a cat-stalked nest. A woman in an apron had a pan raised high above her head and looked as if she meant to use it on a tall man in black. With a start, Mira realized the man was Harry, and her heart nearly leapt out of her chest.

He, however, was quick on his feet and dodged the crazed woman only to be accosted by the butler who took a swing at him. Harry dodged the butler's fist as well and rapped him soundly on the head with the butt of his pistol.

Mira screamed. Why would Harry do such a thing? She called after him but had no hope of being heard for, with a mighty roar, a second woman wearing the keys of a housekeeper at her waist lunged for him just as a thundering from behind Mira threatened to collapse the house. She turned towards the noise to see a dozen footmen dash into the kitchen at a dead run, Sarah Siddons in the lead. With a screech, the monkey vaulted onto the scrub table, into the sink, swung across the greasy wrought iron chandelier in the middle of the room, and landed in a heap on the housekeeper's head, whose ensuing screeches rivaled those of her primate oppressor.

Heedless of the mayhem around him, Harry sprinted for the back door and disappeared into the night. Without a thought except that she could not bear it if she hadn't the chance to speak with him before he disappeared, Mira followed him into the darkness. The sky was heavy with storm clouds and there was little light as she peered across the lawn towards the sea, however, she thought she saw a flash of white on the far side of the lawn just before it winked out of sight. Convinced it was one of Harry's overly-exposed shirt cuffs, she picked up her skirts and ran just as the rain began to fall.

The lawn came to an abrupt halt at the edge of the cliff that overlooked the ocean far below, but Harry was nowhere to be seen. Her skirts and hair whipped tight around her by the wind, she stood and scanned the path that led down to the beach, the rain stinging her face like tiny bits of hail. Then she saw a flash of white in the distance, so far down the path it might as well have been across the ocean. Where was he going? Would he ever return?

The wind in her skirts threatened to blow her from the rocky ridge, but she gathered the fabric into her arms as best she could and flew down the path, the soft, kid leather of her dancing slippers shredding into smaller and smaller pieces with every step. If she did not catch up to him, she knew not what she would do. Nor did she know how she could allow him to leave her if she did. Nearly blinded by the rain, she trained what was left of her vision on the treacherous path, so it came as an utter shock when she ran headlong into him with a thud against his rock-hard chest.

"You little fool!" he ground out, his arm tightening around her with a viselike grip. As instantly as he had locked her in place, he let go and gave her a bit of a shove to the side.

Dazed and more than a little confused, she looked up to find that he held aloft a pistol as close as could be without the muzzle being quite literally in her face. For the briefest of moments she feared he meant to use it against her, but common sense allowed there was no cause, and she realized he pointed it up the path from whence she had just come. Suddenly, a shout rose into the air and the outline of a man came into view as he scampered down the path mere feet from where they stood.

"Mira," Harry growled, his vision trained on the man, "get behind me this instant!

Mira thought it best to do as he said but hadn't a chance to move before another shout came from the path above.

"I know what you are about and I insist you stop immediately!" cried a man in a voice remarkably like that of George.

"Or what, Your Grace?" Harry challenged, stepping in front of Mira. "You shall cudgel me with your stickpin?"

The man had now drawn near enough for Mira to decipher his expression in the inconstant moonlight. "George, surely Papa must have spoken to you by now. I am not yours, and you have no right to treat me thus!"

"I demand that Miss Crenshaw return with me to the house this instant, Haversham! I find your actions heinous, though you are correct in that I have no means to force you from your aim save through my wits."

"You would be better served by the stickpin," Harry quipped. "Am I correct to assume it was you who have been dogging my every step?"

"I admit to having followed you once or twice since your return to England's shores, yes. It was in Miss Crenshaw's best interests."

"Word of my activities abroad seem to have preceded me," Harry said.

"But of course; you are infamous! I couldn't tolerate the thought of Mira being deceived by you but I needed proof before I could hope to dissuade my cousin Anthony from allowing his daughter anywhere near you."

"And did you obtain your proof?"

"Not precisely, but it would seem your secrets do not end with your return to the bosom of your family. Being as I am a fair man, I did try to warn you away."

"Then I was correct in assuming it was you who penned those notes?" Harry demanded.

"What notes?" Mira asked from her position behind Harry's right shoulder.

The ones left here at Cedars, signed anonymous," Harry explained.

"I did not write any such thing!" George cried in a huff.

"Didn't you?" Harry needled.

"No! I left them unsigned. Much more distinguished that way, and by half!"

"All right, then, George," Harry said as if speaking to a particularly dull-witted child. "How is her fate sealed?"

"Need I explain? I should have thought my intentions towards Miss Crenshaw have been made more than clear!" George shouted. "And do put down that gun before some-one gets shot!"

Mira, in possession of a fantastical thought, felt she ought to speak up. "Harry, I believe he thinks us to be elop-ing. By boat!"

Harry lowered the gun just a fraction. "Then you are not in league with Randall and the rest?"

George shook his head. "Randall? No! Who is he?"

"My butler," Harry replied, scanning the path up to the cliff.

"I suppose he is on his way down here to put a stop to this debacle as well, in which case I will be happy to accept his assistance. If you think I shall let you disappear with her, Haversham, you are sadly mistaken! As such, I have alerted the authorities, and they will be here presently. I will *not* be jilted by my own cousin!"

"George, how could you?" Mira cried. "We aren't even officially engaged!"

She was never to know what his response might have been for there came a loud crack, and Harry had her off of her feet and in his arms in the flicker of an eye. As he ran to a dinghy that rested in the sand at the water's edge, understanding dawned and Mira suddenly realized from whence the danger came. "That was a gun! Who is shooting at us?"

Harry jerked his head towards the ridge of the cliff above the path. "That would be a traitor and his compatriots, otherwise known as Randall and the footmen of Cedars, aided and abetted by my cook and housekeeper." He placed Mira on her feet within the confines of the boat, told her to get down, and turned his attention to the men on the ridge of the cliff.

Mira did as she was told, but George would have none of it.

"She will do no such thing," he commanded as he reached into the dinghy and attempted to pull Mira to her feet. "She is coming with me!"

Harry placed a foot into the dinghy to keep it from drifting out to sea. "Don't be a ninny, George! Get off the beach or you'll be shot!"

"Not without Miss Crenshaw," George shouted over the crash of the waves.

Mira rose to her knees to implore her cousin to do as Harry said, but her voice was lost in the crack of a gun as Harry shot into the sand at George's feet who, in turn, lost no time in running headlong down the beach to cower, in relative safety, behind an outcropping of rocks.

There came another shot from the ridge above as Harry pushed the dinghy farther into the waves and jumped inside. As they headed out into the deep water and were tossed about in the waves, Mira wondered if drowning weren't an easier death than being hit by a bullet. Her mind was suddenly filled with all she had heard about the boating accident at Eton, the one everyone spoke of but never explained. She had no clue as to what actually happened, but the consequences must have been grave or it would not have been something of which no one would speak. What had Harry done? Was she doomed to drown if a bullet didn't kill her first?

"Harry," she said, forcing the words through her chattering teeth. "I'm frightened."

He pushed her down into the bottom of the boat in reply, picked up the oars, and began to row. "Just . . . trust me!" he shouted.

What could she say in response? The question of whether or not she trusted him was the one she had given herself to answer often and often, and it was always, eventually and somewhat unaccountably, yes. The clouds shifted, and, for a moment, the moon reflecting on the water provided the light she needed to look into his face as he battled the waves. There was nothing of Bertie there, nothing but the Harry she had known and loved, as well as the Harry she had wished for and newly discovered.

"I do trust you!" she shouted above the roar of the waves and knew he had heard her when his face split into an exultant grin. Warmed by his smile, Mira felt utterly unafraid. She was cold and wet and shivering, but as she glided into her future with the man she loved, she refused to consider any details except that Harry—*her* Harry— returned her love, and they were together.

Another shot rang in the air, and Mira's momentary bliss was shattered. She lifted her head to risk a peek at the shore and saw that it was lined with men who fired upon them relentlessly, their faces illuminated by the sparking of their guns. Most of the bullets landed in the water, but a few bit into the upper prow of the dinghy with an unnerving thunk followed by a vibration Mira could feel through the soles of her feet. Contrary to her fears, Harry was an expert with the oars and he plied them with a strength and urgency she could only admire, until, at long last, it became clear no bullet could possibly reach them and the crisis was over.

Suddenly, Harry tossed down the oars, knelt in the bottom of the boat, and dragged her into his arms. "Mira, my darling Mira, how selfish I am!" he cried, his breath coming in great gasps as he attempted to fill his punished lungs with air. The waves were choppier than ever, and Mira wondered at his enormous strength that kept them both balanced on their knees in the heaving dinghy.

"I couldn't bear to leave you, but I had my orders. Besides, it wasn't safe—*you* weren't safe when you were near me. And then, when you followed me onto the beach . . . perhaps I should have sent you off with George but when faced, once again, with the prospect of leaving you, I simply could not."

With a start, Mira realized he expected a reply to this somewhat confusing speech, however, the moment she opened her mouth, he covered it with his own with a passion entirely new to her. She responded with an answering intensity that shook her to the core while it thrilled her to no end. This was the man she had hungered for, one who could reveal his every feeling and need with trust that she would view his transparency not as weakness, but as a strength, one which she might add to with her own with no fear of rebuff.

"Oh, Harry," she breathed between kisses. "I thought you would never come back to me."

"I never left you," he murmured as he rained kisses to the top of her head. "You were all I thought of."

"But why, Harry? You did come back, but it wasn't *you*. I thought I should die!"

With a groan, he kissed her with lips that were soft, warm, and lingering, and that called to her in ways the demanding kisses hadn't. In spite of the icy rain from above, she felt a glow of warmth spread from her center that radiated out to enclose her entire being with heat. She wanted nothing more than to go on this way forever, but a sliver of rationality remained, one that insisted she ask her questions whilst Harry was inclined to answer them.

"We have wasted so much time!" she professed, pummeling his chest with her fists. "Why did you not come home after Eton?"

It was too dark to read his expression, but the way he released her and slid from his knees to the bottom of the boat told her that the answer pained him. As it was impossible to stay aloft without his support, she took her seat again as well and waited for his voice to come out of the darkness.

"It was the accident, the one at Eton. . . . . I was torn up . . . destroyed, really. And Mother, well . . . the state I was in, I knew I shouldn't have any patience for her. As for my father, he should have proved intolerable."

"But I don't understand; it was just an accident, was it not? What could they have said that would not have been a comfort?"

"My mother and father are never a comfort, no matter the occasion." A brief break in the clouds allowed enough moonlight for her to see the bleakness in his eyes. "Besides, it was my fault," he said in a rush, as if his resolve threatened to desert him, "my fault entirely!"

"Yours!" Mira heard herself exclaim.

"How was I to tell them?" he demanded in a voice that wavered just a little. "They would not have understood how I, their perfect son, could do anything so utterly irresponsible, so foolish, and most of all, so unheroic! It would have served them better had I died attempting to rescue poor Edwin."

"But you did rescue him, and he was quite all right, was he not?"

"He . . . was not," Harry answered, his voice breaking. "He drowned."

"Oh, Harry, I'm so sorry!" she cried, aghast. "But you did *try* to save him."

"Of course I did! Only . . . I failed. That was not the worst of it, however. He was far bigger than I—a veritable giant of a boy—none could blame me for not having the strength to pull him out of the water. Though I tried, Mira, I *did* try!"

"Of course you did!" Mira cried, stretching out her hand in the darkness to touch him in reassurance. "Of course you did!"

"It doesn't matter though. I should never have taken him out on the water. He couldn't swim. I knew that. I *knew* that!" He slammed his fist into the side of the boat.

"Whatever it was that went wrong, it weren't as if you meant for him to drown. It was just an accident."

"Edwin couldn't swim," he repeated with a harsh laugh, "he couldn't row, and he outweighed me by nearly six stone. I had no right to take him out on the water. It was against the rules! It was after vespers and it was dark. God forgive me, it was so dark!"

Mira dreaded to ask but sensed that Harry would not feel absolved until he told her all. "Why *did* you go out on the water at night?"

He covered her hand on his knee with his own. It trembled a little and she felt suddenly cold. Getting to her knees, she crawled to find a place at his side and was gratified when he sighed and put his arm around her shoulders.

"There were these two young ladies," he said in a faint voice, "the nieces of a German prince visiting at Windsor." His head fell back against the edge of the dinghy, and Mira could feel him struggle to control the onset of dry sobs in his chest. She laid her head against his heart which brought his arms instantly around her and his head against hers. "You must believe me, Mira, when I say there was never anyone for me but you! But," he continued after a short silence, "these girls, they were just across the Thames. One day they toured Eton, and Edwin became thoroughly besotted with one of them. Things rather took off from there."

Mira backed her hand into the palm of his, rolled his fingers firm within her own, and pulled them tight beneath her chin. "Surely you were as besotted as he," she prompted, surprised at how much she hurt at the question even as she wondered how she would abide the answer.

Harry reached for her other hand and drew it to his lips, kissing it with sincere fervency. "Not with her; her sister, the one with the long, red curls. She put me so much in mind of you," he said, his voice shaking. "I missed you so much. I missed Prospero Park, your brothers, your parents. I missed being known, truly *known*, rather than treated as a chess piece on a board. In point of fact," he said, his voice stronger now, "I was unutterably lonely, and Edwin was my only friend. When these girls managed to get a message to us, it was so unexpected and terribly clever; I never did learn how they pulled it off."

"So it was Edwin's idea to go out after dark and row across the Thames to Windsor Castle," Mira supplied.

"No, it was mine. Forgive me, Mira, it was mine!"

She was astonished by how much his admission pained her. "But why? Surely you hadn't expected to enter Windsor Castle and find these girls without being discovered!"

"We were young. We were determined. And now you know why I couldn't come back, not to my parents and not to . . . not to *you*."

Mira thought of how he must have felt, alone on the water at night, on an elicit errand, his friend drowned, his entire future hanging in the balance. "Oh, Harry," she breathed, "however did you manage?"

"I lied," he said matter-of-factly, "about why we were out. As for the rest, there are benefits to being a seventeen-year-old lord. The authorities made sure my dear *pere et mere* never knew the more unsavory details, and, come the end of term a fortnight later, I was advised to put as much time and distance as possible between myself and the consequences of my actions. Naturally, I did just that but, oh, how I longed for a *tete-a-tete* with your good father. I should have liked to have had his wise advice."

"And what of me?" Mira asked in a voice faint with dread. "Did you not long to see me?"

She felt his answer as he shook his head against hers. "I couldn't. It wasn't a matter of wanting or not wanting—I simply couldn't."

Harry's pain along with her own was almost too much to bear. Her heart felt as if it were breaking, but she knew she hadn't the whole of it as of yet. "But, Harry, why so long? Shouldn't a mere six months or a year have served as well?"

He drew a deep breath, as if he had been without air for quite some time, followed by a small sob as he caught her more tightly in his arms. "That? *That* is what you wish to know?" he asked, his voice full of awed disbelief. "Are you to say that you forgive me?"

"Forgive you? For what? For pulling a school-boy prank that went awry? For being lonely? For wishing to feel happy when you were so miserable? No," she said and attempted to shake her head under the weight of his. "There is nothing to forgive in that."

He made no response and was silent so long she began to wonder if perhaps she had said something terribly wrong. "Harry, what is it? What would you have me say?"

He drew a ragged breath, and his arms trembled as he pulled her closer. "That you regard me as more than the friend of your girlhood, or even a man who should make you a suitable husband, but as the very one essential to your happiness."

Mira pulled back to look him in the face as fully as the fluctuating moonlight would allow. "Harry Haversham! When I stepped into this boat, I thought I would as likely drown as not. I followed you down that jagged, craggy, treacherous path in the first place so as to beg you not to leave me! How can you possibly doubt that I would rather die than be without you?"

"My dearest girl," he breathed as he once again pulled her close. To her consternation, he began to shake; she thought perhaps it was from the cold until his tears fell hot against her icy head. "What can I have done to deserve such love?" he murmured. "But will your parents so forgive my sins? Might they, in good conscience, give you into my care? And, if not, will your love of me outlast their displeasure?"

"Yes! Oh, Harry, yes! When we return and explain it all to them, both about the accident and why you have been behaving so strangely, they will understand, if you but tell the truth. Perhaps you do not wish to tell me all your secrets but surely you might trust Papa! Let us return to Cedars this very minute, and you will see for yourself how very kind he will be."

"No, Mira," he said as he took her by the shoulders and turned her to face him. The storm had abated, and the clouds parted so as to reveal the gravity of his expression. "Neither of us can go back just yet. You have seen those men, seen their faces. You have the power to send them to the gallows. Should we return before they are apprehended, your life would not be worth a farthing, which is about what mine has been worth since my return to England."

"Oh," Mira breathed as the truth of his words bore down on her. "Those men—all this time you have been trying to stop them. But from what?"

"I am not free to tell you," he said as he smoothed the wet hair from her brow. "For now all I can say is that I must deliver an important letter."

Mira was reminded of what Harry had almost said back at the inn, about his being in service to the Queen. From Mira's vantage point in the boat in the middle of the ocean, it seemed quite plausible indeed. "Of course, Harry, I will wait and promise not to pester you with any more questions pertaining to such things. But what of my family? Are they safe? What if they heard the commotion and ran outside? Will those terrible men not shoot at any who try to stop them?"

"I'm afraid there is naught we can do, Mira. We must leave their fates in George's hands for the present."

"George? You can't be serious!"

"Indeed, quite serious. Did he not inform us he had alerted the authorities in order to prevent our supposed elopement? With any luck, they have long since arrived on the scene. When we have gained land, we shall seek word that it is so, and your duke will doubtless be lauded as a great hero.

"Not my duke. My Viscount Haversham!" she insisted, smiling into his eyes.

He favored her with an intent look in response, one so like the heated gaze she remembered from the drawing room at Prospero Park only a week and a lifetime ago. Without any warning, he put his hands around her waist and lifted her from the bottom of the boat to sit on the bench. Removing his jacket, he put it around her shoulders to ward off the chill air, knelt before her, and took her hands in his.

chapter sixteen

The moment had arrived, the one which would determine Harry's fate for all the years to come. He had dreamed about it many times since he had departed for the Continent, even as far back as Eton, but never truly believed he deserved her enough to petition her with such a request. But now he knew she loved him—*loved* him!—just as he loved her. It was nothing short of a miracle.

"Mira," he said, renewing his grip on her hands. "I now must ask of you my own question. I confess, I do not deserve a favorable answer, not when I have concealed the truth from you with regard to a great many things."

"Oh, but Harry, it is not your fault!" Mira cried.

"Isn't it? I might have chosen to come home long before I swore my allegiance to any other than you. I should have trusted in you, in your generosity, in the capacity of your enormous heart. We might have been together, at Prospero Park, while I waited on you to become of age rather than you being compelled to wait on me. I might," he added, his voice wavering, "have given you the opportunity to be true to me, even if I have not always been entirely true to you."

She made no reply in his defense. As her eyes grew wide and filled with tears, he felt as if the wind had been knocked out of him, yet he knew he deserved far more censure than she had offered. There was naught left to do but ask; perhaps she would be merciful.

"So," he said, taking a deep breath. "I beg of you the answer to a question I have longed to ask every minute of every hour of every day since my return to England. Will you, Miss Miranda Crenshaw, make this wretched man happier than he deserves and agree to be my wife?"

"Yes!" she cried without a moment's hesitation. "Oh, Harry, I thought you would never ask!"

Harry resisted the impulse to jump to his feet and whoop for joy; he would have her think about her choice before he accepted her answer. "Despite how I have wronged you?"

"It is in the past," she said, shaking her head vehemently. "We need never speak of it again."

"And what of the weakness of my father and the foolishness of my mother?" he pressed.

To his great surprise, Mira laughed. "I will have you know I've been thinking on how to sort her out ever since we arrived at Cedars. Did you realize she left your father at home so as to make a grand entrance in the arms of another man?"

"I fail to find anything promising in that speech," he said with a moan.

"I must confess I had thought you would take her in hand. I believe you made a heroic attempt," she rushed to assure him. "Yet I eventually concluded the matter required a woman's mind to anticipate what would deter her from her folly."

"Pray tell!" Harry demanded, doubtful, but amused.

"You *will* laugh at me, Harry, but I am persuaded she will prove most easily managed when we have a babe we might hold over her head. She will not dare displease us if we keep her grandchild from her. And when the novelty wears off, well . . . ," she hesitated, suddenly shy, "there will be another for her to dote upon."

"A babe," he mused, both awed by her wisdom and humbled by her optimism. "I do believe you are correct! How utterly perspicacious of you!" he said with a squeeze to her fingers. "To claim you as mine feels like a boon too big to take in, but children . . . I had not thought that far, but, yes, a babe will do very nicely and the sooner the better!"

Despite the fickle moonlight, he fancied her cheeks burned under his ardent gaze and he marveled yet again that she would find it in her heart to love him. It made it so much more difficult to ask his next question. "What of your parents' objections? They will suffer much when you don't return. They might be less inclined to look favorably upon me when they learn what has happened."

Mira's smile vanished and she lowered her eyes. "Yes, it is as you say. But they shall eventually see that it is for the best as there are bound to be rumors. Who knows when we shall be free to return, and there will be those who say we have run off together. There will also be others, perhaps George and his mother, who will claim you were forced to marry me against your will."

She withdrew her hands from his and placed them on either side of his face. "If you have only offered for me out of duty, you must pick up those oars and take me to shore this very instant for I would rather be shot dead by that traitorous butler than make you unhappy."

"Mira, my love, I wished to wring your neck when you ran onto that beach; I wanted you safe, out of harm's way.

But now I must confess that you were the wiser of us two. It doesn't matter to me if we marry in haste or at leisure, at home or abroad, as long as I am no danger of losing you, I have nothing of which to complain."

"Well, now that we are agreed on that score," Mira said brightly, "what can be done about the fact that we are far from shore in a dinghy, wet, cold, hungry, and tired?"

"Never fear," he said with a smile of delight, that, try as he might, he could not hold back. "You must merely turn about."

Mira looked doubtful but turned around to fill her vision with what Harry could already see: a man in military dress stood at the prow of a large ship, holding aloft the only onboard point of light as it slipped towards them through the misty night.

"Is that for us?" Mira asked in suitable awe.

"Yes, indeed. What do you think?"

"I think it marvelous! Where are we going?"

"Wherever you wish as long as it is outside of England. At least for the present," he said, his foolish grin growing wider and wider every moment. He could hardly believe his life was headed in exactly the direction he desired most, in spite of all that might have happened to prevent it.

"It doesn't matter to me where," Mira urged. "As long as we can get a message to Mama and Papa assuring them of my safety, I am most happy to follow you anywhere—but only as your wife. How long before we may be married?"

Harry looked into her eager face and felt his heart turn over. "Just as soon as we have landed somewhere safe, notified your parents, procured a license, and acquired suitable attire in which to be wed," he outlined. "Is that soon enough for you?" he gently chided.

"I suppose it will have to do," she said with a tiny frown. "Though I am persuaded the captain of that ship might marry us in a trice."

Harry thought it a brilliant notion and was surprised to hear himself object. "Mira, you can't mean it. If we wait, your parents should be able to join us. You wish them to attend your wedding, do you not?"

"It is not my mama and papa who concern me. If only you knew what your mother has planned for your wedding day, you would quake in your boots! It is best you marry me this very night. What say you to that, Harry Haversham?"

"I say, I could kiss you!" Harry cried, words being the furthest thing from his mind.

Mira glanced back at the ship as it tacked steadily closer. "How long before they catch up to us?" she asked.

"Long enough for as many kisses as you wish," Harry murmured, his lips already in her hair and poised for travel.

"Oh, Harry, you *have* come back to me," she sighed as she melted into his arms and surrendered to his advance.

Made in the USA
Middletown, DE
28 April 2017